Rena shook her head as she continued, "Marriage ought to mean more than that."

The sternness on Ford's face didn't change by a flicker. "It should mean more than that, but often doesn't. It ought to mean more than lust and bringing a new generation into the world. But most times it *is* about convenient sex and having kids."

"What about...love?" The question had come out almost without Rena's permission. She knew Ford wanted the land and he'd marry her without a second thought to get it.

A wedding dilemma:

What should a sexy, successful bachelor do if he's too busy
making millions to find a wife? Or if he finds the perfect
woman, and just *has* to strike a bridal bargain…

The perfect proposal:

The solution? For better, for worse, these grooms in a hurry
have decided to sign, seal and deliver the ultimate
marriage contract…to *buy* a bride!

Will these paper marriages blossom into wedded bliss?

Don't miss our next CONTRACT BRIDES story
in Harlequin Romance®:

Strategy for Marriage (#3707)
by Margaret Way
on-sale July 2002

MARRIAGE ON DEMAND

Susan Fox

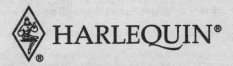

TORONTO • NEW YORK • LONDON
AMSTERDAM • PARIS • SYDNEY • HAMBURG
STOCKHOLM • ATHENS • TOKYO • MILAN • MADRID
PRAGUE • WARSAW • BUDAPEST • AUCKLAND

For my good friend and fellow author, Kathy Carmichael:
Thanks for your friendship, sense of humor and insight.

ISBN 0-373-03696-5

MARRIAGE ON DEMAND

First North American Publication 2002.

CHAPTER ONE

EVEN for a woman who'd endured emotional hardship her whole life in hope of at last gaining her father's affection and approval, it was an incredible mandate: *You'll marry Ford Harlow.*

Rena Lambert stood on the open porch that morning at the back of the Lambert Ranch house, so stunned by her father's terse decree that she felt lightheaded. Dread gripped her insides. Disbelief made it hard to speak in the quiet, careful way she always had to the bitter, volatile man who'd never shown a smidgen of tenderness. If he'd ever felt any.

"Years past time for you to marry," he said, then let his hard gaze slice critically over her from head to boot before it shifted dismissively away.

"I have no interest in ma—"

Her father's impatient words cut her off. "Folks already talk. You're a mannish female with no natural feelings. Men don't want a woman who's better at being a man than she is at being female."

The blunt words sent a wave of pain and humiliation through her that made her face feel stiff and on fire. All Rena's life, Abner Lambert had scorned any show of femininity or weakness in his daughter. To berate her now for repressing the natural inclinations he'd always been so vocal and unsparing about was the height of cruelty.

She recognized the familiar sting of frustrated tears, but the rigid emotional control she'd practiced since early childhood kept her eyes dry. Heat gathered behind them until they burned.

Rena Lambert had grown up with the knowledge that her birth had caused the death of the only woman her father had ever cared for. And she'd been born female, which meant Abner had no son to carry on his legacy. A son might have earned her father's love, or at least his respect, by virtue of being male and capable of carrying on the family name her father was so rabidly proud of.

The fact that he'd never chosen to remarry and have other children who might have been sons was beneath his consideration. Blaming Rena had been much more satisfying to his twisted sense of justice than assigning himself responsibility for his own choices.

But what about her choices? Perhaps she'd become as twisted as he. How else could she account for her lifelong pursuit of approval and acceptance?

Dimly she realized that her craving for her father's approval was connected to the guilt he'd instilled in her. Guilt craved redemption, but false guilt craved it more obsessively.

Rena stared at her father's harshly carved profile as he went on, each word just as cruel and devastating as the others.

"Won't let a female inherit Lambert. Your first son'll get all that's mine. Harlow'll oversee it till the boy's old enough to take over. If you can't bear sons, the ranch'll go to Frank Casey or one of his boys."

Now he aimed a hard glance at her shock-frozen expression. "That happens, you'd better have something Harlow'll want to keep you around for, 'cause he'll already have what he bargained to get."

And he won't need you. It was some surprise that he hadn't actually said it out loud, but he knew he'd communicated his meaning precisely.

"Harlow wants you at his place tonight at seven. Informal supper, he said."

Shame and hurt roared so high then that it was a miracle she could stand so quietly and keep her composure. Her tone was carefully mild.

"The two of you have it all worked out," she dared softly. "But why saddle him with me? Let him buy the west section. Will the ranch to Frank and his sons. They've worked hard for you and they're loyal."

She'd worked just as hard, labored harder than any man who'd ever given his sweat and blood to Lambert land. She'd hoped to someday inherit the ranch she loved, but suddenly the last true hope behind every effort in her life vanished in this new toxic flood of her father's relentless bitterness.

How could she have believed that his grudge against her would someday ease? Or that she'd ever been worth more to him than an extra pair of hands to do the work? Her father went on and she felt herself sway with dizziness.

"Figure I owe you that much, since you can't seem to get a man's interest on your own."

Old fury burst up and burned wildly for several hot moments, but she rigidly held it back, though the very pressure of it made her feel strangled. Rena didn't care that the faint curve of her lips revealed the depth of her own bitterness and disillusionment.

Without a word, she turned away to cross the porch and let herself into the house. Her throat pounded so hard that she wondered dazedly if she might faint.

Like a robot, she walked up the back stairs, the sound of her boots as subdued as she felt. Once in her room, she methodically set about the task of packing her things.

She should have left this place the day she'd turned eighteen. She should have left this *hell*. What kind of female could have lived so long with this? How many men *would* have?

Men don't want a woman who's better at being a man than she is at being female.

Her father was wrong. She wasn't truly better at being a man. Most men wouldn't have put up with such treatment, much less borne up under the weight and agony of it. Most men had more self-respect. All men had more pride.

Her own stubborn refusal to relinquish hope suddenly seemed pitiful. How many times did you let someone smash your fingers with a hammer before you had sense enough to move your hand?

Though she'd realized the truth long ago, she'd not let herself acknowledge it. Her days—years of them—had amounted to little more than waking up in the morning and pushing herself through each day, weathering the blistering desert of rejection and frustrated hope until exhaustion drove her to bed at night to dream foolish dreams of better times.

How many men who were worth a damn to anyone or to themselves would have been reduced to that?

The sudden need to put an end to that insanity— to at last show some spine and pride—sent a fierce new fire through her as she got boxes from the attic and put stack after stack of clothing from her dresser into them.

Ford Harlow was surely under the impression that he was shackling himself to a female no one else would want so he could get access to a piece of land he'd coveted for years. Just the idea that her father had gone to him to propose such a bizarre notion sent a fresh surge of humiliation scorching over her from scalp to toe.

What kind of man was Ford Harlow? She'd thought better of him than to fall in with the twisted plans of a hateful old man out to buy a husband for his "mannish" daughter. How had he taken her father's proposal? Had he laughed?

In the end, he'd evidently accepted it. But to get a piece of land, not a wife. She wondered if he'd truly agreed to the part about fathering a son.

The delicate shame she recognized as purely female was the next agony she had to endure. For years, she'd taken vigilant care to never reveal that she had a crush on Ford Harlow. Her father would have verbally savaged her for showing interest in any man, particularly a man of Ford Harlow's caliber.

And it would have mortified her if Ford himself had ever detected it. The few times he'd had occasion to speak to her, he'd been kind, almost gentle, though his rugged looks and terse manner intimidated her. She'd responded coolly to him and kept herself aloof, but her wounded ego had been soothed by his attention, and profoundly flattered. That her heart would respond to him had been as natural as it had been impossible to prevent.

She couldn't bear for a man like him to think she'd been a willing—no, an *eager*—party to her father's scheme. She knew worldly, compelling men like

Ford Harlow barely noticed that sexless females like her existed. It was shocking to think he might have taken her father's scheme to marry her off to him seriously. At least seriously enough to accept the deal and set a time to speak to her about it.

She had to see him now, she had to put a stop to this. But, oh God, how could she face him?

Not giving herself time to shrink from the task of countering the excruciating shame of what her father had done, Rena abandoned the growing collection of belongings and walked shakily out of her room to do just that before she lost her nerve.

The new stallion Ford Harlow had spent a fortune on was fractious and volatile, with a host of surly habits that had been tolerated and indulged by his last owner.

The shout that went up at the stud barn had drawn his attention and he left the colt he was about to work to head down the alley that bisected that section of corrals. He'd nearly reached the stud barn, when the blood-red stallion burst from the open doors into the sunshine, defying the efforts of the two men who were trying to get a hand on his lead rope. Two more men rushed from their work to block the animal's path, but the wily stallion dodged them and shot away.

Obviously the qualities that made him a stand-out—brains, ability and speed—had facilitated his escape. Ford rushed to intercept the powerful horse, but the red devil charged on, boldly knocking him out of the way. The lead rope he'd managed to snag burned through his palm and fingers before it snapped free.

Ford swore, but as he started after the stallion, he caught sight of the slender female who'd apparently just walked through the stable from the driveway on the other side.

Rena Lambert was a striking presence against the shade-darkened interior of the stable behind her. Tall and slender, her body had the sort of feminized athletic fitness beneath her plaid shirt and jeans that spoke volumes about how hard she worked.

She was also all female, though she acted anything but. She probably never suspected the prurient thoughts men had about her lushly rounded attributes and her long, leanly muscled legs.

Her move to intercept the runaway was as graceful as the woman herself, but Ford felt a jolt of alarm as she stepped calmly into the stallion's path.

The animal reacted instantly, as if he'd been startled by something in her movement, though Ford had detected nothing. The red animal skidded wildly to a stop and shifted direction only to nearly run through the board fence on one side of the alley, before he feinted back to catch Rena off guard or to bully her into letting him pass.

Ford was running now to intervene, but the big horse suddenly reared, practically on top of the slim woman who didn't so much as flinch.

It was over in those next tense seconds. Rena Lambert never showed even a flicker of fear or hesitation as the stallion's front hooves started down only a few inches from her right shoulder. She merely shifted to the side to catch the flipping end of the lead rope.

The stallion squealed as his hooves hit the dirt, but before he could bunch his powerful hindquarters to bolt, Rena used her grip on the lead rope to haul his big head around and force him to circle.

Caught off guard, the stallion whipped around her as if eager to participate. Ford halted within a few feet of the pair, watching tensely as Rena used nothing but her grip on the heavy lead and her hand on the stallion's flank to urge him to keep moving in the small, tight circle. The low-level cloud of dust they kicked up quickly obscured Ford's ability to keep track of the fast-paced dance.

Seconds later, the horse dramatically slowed then abruptly came to a halt. The stallion lowered his head and let out the kind of long snort that signaled surrender and calm. Rena gave him a firm pat on his damp neck and murmured a few quiet words.

Not once had she shouted, not once had she done anything to cause the big animal pain. In essence, she'd merely taken over and redirected the animal's energy while neatly demonstrating her own authority over him until he'd let her know he'd had enough.

The pleasure of seeing her do that sharpened Ford's interest. He'd not expected to see her before tonight, but he knew right away why she'd shown up early. The high, hot color that surged up her cheeks as he approached confirmed it.

"Much obliged." He took the lead rope she passed him. Her incredible blue gaze with its thick fringe of black lashes shifted from his and the color in her face deepened.

For another woman, that would have been coy and flirtatious. But Rena Lambert was neither of those. She was aloof—painfully aloof—and quiet in a way that fairly shouted proof that her father frequently berated her.

It was no secret that the old man was an SOB, and that he treated his only child like dirt. Ford wondered why she took it. Did she think she deserved it or had Abner undermined her so much that she was afraid to go out into the world on her own?

Ford had only tolerated Abner's visit yesterday because Rena intrigued him. He'd learned nothing that truly satisfied his curiosity, but he'd been shocked by what Abner Lambert meant to do to his daughter.

The injustice of that was far sharper for Ford than the personal insult of having a crazy old man use a piece of land to buy a husband for his daughter.

And why the hell would he need to? Rena was beautiful. Her dark, glossy hair came down just past her collar, but it was thick and lustrous and straight. Her face was an intriguing mix of high cheekboned beauty and common symmetry. Her nose was fine and straight and her mouth had a vulnerability to it that asked a man to go slow.

Combined with a close-up view of the rest of her, Rena Lambert was a pleasure to look at. The lustful feelings he'd felt toward her in the past impacted him more deeply and forcefully than ever now. The notion that he might have to marry her wasn't exactly distasteful.

But instinct warned him to conceal that. She was already here to put a stop to her father's scheme. Any hint of personal interest from him would scare her away, and he wasn't yet certain what he truly wanted, other than a parcel of land.

"I wasn't expecting to see you until tonight," he said, unable to take his eyes from her.

Her blue gaze shifted to his when he spoke, but dropped away almost instantly.

"I can't...have supper with you. I—" She cut herself off as the two ranch hands from the stud barn arrived to collect the stallion.

Rena's nerves were jumping painfully high now that the moment had come to speak to Ford Harlow. She was tall for a woman, but Ford made her feel petite and feminine. He wasn't peacock handsome, but he was rugged and compelling. So compelling that she felt the power of his dark gaze on her every second.

The long-repressed femininity she rarely acknowledged was clamoring at his nearness. Men didn't normally affect her, but something about Ford's masculinity pulled at her.

A peculiar feeling that was half excitement, half fear sparkled sweetly through her and she tried desperately to suppress it. She was terrified her reaction to him would show, because something in his nearly black gaze hinted at unerring perception. She wasn't used to men like him. The men she worked with every day accepted her presence, but nothing in their manner or in the way they spoke to her had ever seemed personal.

Every look Ford gave her, every word he spoke, somehow seemed intensely personal, as if he meant to catch her notice, as if he was either probing for something or trying to coax it out of her. It was terrifying, it was flattering, it was profoundly confusing.

It dawned on her then that she'd let several moments go by without finishing the sentence she'd cut off when Ford's men had led the stallion away. Her gaze shot back to see the calmness in his. He was waiting for her, watching her steadily and the peculiar feeling of excitement and fear soared higher.

"Pardon me," she said hastily to apologize for the brief wait, then struggled to keep from fidgeting as she went on, determined to get it out. "My father just told me about…"

Her heart quailed with dread. She glanced away from him, seeking relief from the sharp search his dark eyes made of hers.

"About what my father asked, I had nothing to do with that," she told him. "I refuse to let him…"

The frustration of wanting to declare her intentions without saying too much about her true relationship with her father made it difficult. Her gaze shifted back to Ford's just in time to see him step toward her and reach for her arm.

"Let's go to the house, Miz Lambert, get something cool to drink. We can talk there."

Rena froze that second before his strong fingers closed warmly around her arm. She tried not to flinch, but she couldn't seem to control that. She couldn't control the sudden, baffling weakness of her legs as she turned with him to start through the stable to go to the house.

She'd had no fear of the runaway stallion, no worries about standing her ground and catching his lead to calm him down, but she was terrified of this, so terrified. And the grimness about Ford now further unsettled her.

Could he feel the small earthquake his touch set off? The pleasure-fear of his warm grip surged so strongly that the moment they were through the stable, she pulled her arm away. Horrified that the awkward movement suggested she couldn't bear his touch another moment, she faltered to a halt. So did he, and his calm gaze fastened on hers.

Her mouth went dry with bad nerves and it was a struggle to get the words out.

"I mean no offense to you, Mr. Harlow. What my father suggested…I won't be part of that. Good day."

She cringed inwardly at the stiff way it had come out, particularly the clumsy formality of that last. *Good day.* Fake-sounding and pretentious in a way that sent heat to her face and a sick feeling to her stomach. And she'd meant to say it then walk to her pickup and leave, but her legs were trembling and she couldn't seem to move.

The sick feeling deepened as Ford's expression went grim. Her worked up emotions felt the shock of the sudden change all the way to her feet.

"The drought's getting worse, Ms. Lambert. I need the water on that west section."

The drought of the past two years had depleted water resources in that part of Texas. Lambert Ranch had also been affected, but it was still water rich. Enough so that her father could let that west section go to Ford Harlow and still have plenty.

"Make my father an offer, but ask to lease the land. He's cutting back on stock, so the cash will come in handy."

It was a confidential bit of information that caused her a strong pang of guilt, but the truth was Abner was growing more difficult to work with, and he now had trouble keeping good ranch hands. Hence the cutback in livestock.

Ford's stern expression hardened even more and for the first time, Rena got a clear glimpse of harshness and implacability. The kindness she'd seen in him before suddenly seemed as much a rippling mist above hard pavement as any other mirage.

She realized then that her secret fantasies about this man had been just as foolish and naive as her hope that her father would at last approve of her. She should have guessed that Ford Harlow was a harsh, implacable man. He was successful and he ruled his own small Texas empire. There could be no true softness in him, no sign of anything that wasn't domineering and driven for him to be able to rule over so much and several other business interests as well. She'd always been intimidated by him, but she'd not thought it was due to more than his rugged good looks or his terse, no-nonsense manner.

She'd been wrong. Particularly after what she'd grown up with, she should have been able to see Ford Harlow for what he was: a man like her father. Not emotionally twisted like Abner—at least she hoped not—but hard and driven to have the world bow down at a finger snap. A man who felt entitled to get his way however it affected lesser mortals.

Nothing changed on Ford's stern face, so she added more. "Ask him to lease you the land. He'll will Lambert Ranch to Frank Casey, and Frank will likely need to sell off that section to pay inheritance taxes. There's no reason for…" Her voice choked to a whisper and she felt her face heat. "No reason for you—"

She cut herself off and glanced away to finish it. "People don't do that kind of thing anymore. At least, not where it's civilized."

The silence between them thundered in her ears. God help her, she didn't have the courage to both wait for his comment and watch his stern face while he said it.

"People do still do it, Ms. Lambert. Your father and I aren't quite done negotiating, but I expect you and I could join the ranks of the uncivilized any day now."

Rena's gaze shot back to his solemn look. Her soft, "No," was as choked with disbelief as it was spontaneous.

"The forecast is skimpy on rain and I'm tired of hauling in water at a premium price."

Rena shook her head, now unable to tear her gaze away from the rocky sternness of his rugged face. "You can't marry a stranger for a piece of land. Marriage ought to mean more than that."

The sternness on his face didn't change by a flicker. "It should mean more than that, but often doesn't. It ought to mean more than lust and it ought to mean more than bringing a new generation into the world. But most times it *is* about convenient sex and having kids."

"What about...love?" It was a bold and intimate question for her to ask, but it had come out almost without her permission.

Now his stern mouth relaxed into a faint curve. "You are young, aren't you." It wasn't a question. "And naive. Besides which, Abner's in an almighty hurry and I'm not sure the drought gives us time for more than an agreement and a ceremony."

He hadn't truly answered her question, or had he? What he was saying was that his mind was made up. He wanted the land and he'd marry her without a second thought to get it.

Convenient sex and having kids. Apparently those were his only requirements beyond getting his hands on the west section of Lambert Ranch. Why that caused her incredible pain was no surprise to a woman who'd had so little love in her life that she'd fantasized about having at least a little someday.

Disappointment made her heart quiver and feel heavy. Her soft, "I'm packing to leave today" was little more than a whisper. She couldn't seem to control the sad undertone in her words, so she finished quickly. "Your business is with my father, not me."

She turned to start for her pickup and escape, but Ford's voice brought her to an abrupt halt.

"I'm still negotiating with your father. He either wills Lambert to you outright, or there's no deal."

Startled by that, Rena looked back at him. "What?"

The stern line of his mouth curved slightly, but the dark glitter in his eyes banished any impression of humor. "You heard right. I'd be getting more than a wife, so you should get more than a husband. And just so you know, no man's going to devalue my wife to the level of brood mare."

It took a few seconds for her to absorb that, and she searched his face, looking for any sign that she'd misheard. Hadn't he just said that marriage often didn't mean more than convenient sex and having children? So why would he now say something that seemed opposite that? And something that so strongly hinted at a streak of protectiveness and maybe possessiveness?

"Tell Abner I'll be by later," he continued, as if he was oblivious to her reaction, though she knew he must have sensed it. "If things don't work out and you go through with your plan to leave, I might have a job for you. See if you're as good with horses as people say." He paused and his voice lowered to a gravelly drawl. "I suspect they're right."

A compliment. Rena didn't know how to take it, she didn't know how to take any of the astonishing things he'd said to her. The rush of pleasure—profound pleasure—was unfamiliar and she was suddenly incapable of doing more than keeping her reaction under rigid control. Her face felt like a stiff mask.

Her perception—that Ford Harlow was a man like her father—had abruptly reversed. The odd sense that he was on her side and that when he saw her father he would be her advocate, was astonishing. No one had taken her side against her father since before her aunt's death when she was eight.

A whisper of trust gusted over her heart, but the offer of a job was almost as terrifying as the thought of marrying him. Anything that would amount to being near this man on a regular basis was terrifying. And exciting.

She prayed her soft, "I'll tell him," didn't reveal anything deeper than her agreement to tell her father to expect his arrival. She still couldn't respond to the rest of what he'd said. Seconds rushed on and she felt them acutely. The best she could do was give him a faint nod and turn away to walk to her pickup.

CHAPTER TWO

THE Lambert Ranch west section had once been a ranch of its own, and though Harlow ancestors had bought up other properties further west, the original owner had sold the piece to a Lambert. On a modern-day map, the parcel would look like a hefty bite into the eastern boundary of Harlow Ranch.

In the time it had taken Rena to pack her things from the house and load everything into her pickup, she'd decided that Ford had changed his mind. He'd probably elected to wait for Frank Casey and his sons to inherit. Besides, Harlow Ranch was already vast. The most the parcel would add to it besides more grazing and water, was a straighter eastern boundary.

Given that, there was no logical reason for Ford Harlow to go to the extreme of shackling himself to a woman he barely knew, particularly a female who was far less than a man like him should have to settle for. Desperation might put a man in that situation, but Ford was hardly desperate. The drought was a drain on his resources, but little more. Other than the challenge of bargaining to at last get the section, there could be no other reason than greed or ego to marry her to get it.

And, if greed or ego was the reason, marrying a woman whom everyone considered mannish and un-desirable was hardly the kind of showy marriage match expected of such a man.

Because she'd assumed Ford had changed his mind, his arrival was a surprise, but it was a shock when he insisted that she be present during his ne-gotiations with her father.

That negotiation quickly degraded to a virtual showdown. The tension in the den was excruciating, though it was mostly hers. Her father sat stiffly be-hind his desk, his ongoing irritation evident. Ford leaned back comfortably in one of the wing chairs that his size seemed to dwarf, one booted ankle rest-ing casually on the opposite knee. Rena was too jit-tery to sit and stood at the side of the room.

Her father, in a perpetual black mood, glared across the desk at the man who gave every impres-sion of being untroubled by the old man's increasing surliness.

Abner's voice was sharp. "You want the land bad enough, you'll marry the girl."

Ford let a moment pass, as if to emphasize what he was about to say. Abner leaned forward, drawn by his impatience for a response.

"If I marry your daughter, she'll be my legal wife. I won't let my wife suffer a slight that's in my power to prevent, and I won't profit by a marriage that won't also profit her.''

Ford's solemn declaration sent a flush of anger to her father's face. ''And I can put in my will that no Harlow can ever get that land,'' he railed. ''Frank Casey'll have to abide by that, so she's your only chance to get it.''

Ford was unperturbed by the threat. ''The land is yours, do what you want with it. But you need to realize you've given her no reason to give me the time of day.''

The old man hit the desk with his fist. ''She'll marry you because she does what I say.''

''She's packed to leave, Abner, so it's clear you've lost any say over her.''

Now Abner shot Rena a furious look. ''She'll get a husband outta this deal she'd never get otherwise.''

Rena did her best to appear unfazed by yet another of her father's insults. She was already impatient to leave the room and be on her way. She might have left the room that moment, but Ford spoke.

''How do you know I couldn't win her over and persuade her to marry me?'' The hard look on Ford's face said he'd taken Abner's remark as an insult to his romantic abilities as a man, rather than the way her father had meant it: that Rena couldn't get a husband unless her father bribed one.

Abner seemed confused for a moment, then

flushed as he understood Ford's interpretation of his
remark. Rena felt a rare spurt of amusement and relaxed the tiniest bit. Ford went on.

"The only one you need to lure into this deal is
your daughter."

The old man got to his feet. "She's got no business turnin' it down as it stands."

"She's smarter than that. You put it in writing that
she inherits Lambert, and I'll marry her to get the
west section signed over to me right away."

The profanities her father spewed for those next
seconds weren't a surprise to Rena, and evidently not
to Ford either, who seemed untroubled by them.
Abner finished with a furious, "What do I get outta
this?"

The question spoke volumes to Rena. What Abner
would have gotten under the terms of his proposal
was another way to slight his only child and the satisfaction of putting her in a situation with the potential to cause her hurt.

Rena was hardly surprised by that, but it shamed
her now that she'd stayed so long with someone who
bore her such ill will.

"You get control over who she marries," Ford
answered smoothly.

"I can marry her off to anybody," Abner railed
back.

Ford smiled then, but there was something calculating about it. "Will Lambert pride be satisfied by just anybody? Or did you choose me because a Harlow's considered a worthy match for a Lambert? What about that son you wanted her to have? Will just anybody have the pedigree to suit you?"

It was either a brilliant argument that played up to Abner's pride or a sign of ego and arrogance.

Just so you know, I won't let any man devalue my wife to the level of brood mare. The talk of a worthy match and a pedigree seemed to contradict that declaration, but the abrupt absence of bad temper in Abner as he appeared to give the argument serious consideration suggested that whatever Ford's true opinion was, he'd managed to target the one thing that might give her a chance to directly inherit Lambert Ranch.

He'd also managed to completely distract her father from his grudge against her. Rena held her breath. She'd seen her father's ability to reason deteriorate these past years, but this was the first time she'd seen anyone use it against him.

She immediately felt guilty for the satisfaction she felt, though years of her father's cruelty made it impossible to not be a little glad to see someone use his pride to manipulate him.

"All right."

Rena felt the room tilt a bit as she stared at her father and heard his words.

Abner gave a decisive nod and repeated, ''All right. She inherits.''

''I'll need to see a will and I want the details in writing by the end of the week. I'll marry your daughter the day the land deed is signed over.''

Her father's cranky look returned. ''That's four days.''

''We should be able to get a marriage license by then, and I want the deal on the section settled.'' Ford glanced her way and she struggled to keep her expression impassive. ''Unless she wants more time to plan a wedding.''

Quiet satisfaction glinted in Ford's dark gaze. He'd bargained with her father and won. He'd done what he'd set out to do and he gave no sign that he expected her to refuse the deal.

And how could she? She'd toiled for years in hope of one day inheriting the land that was her birthright. She'd endured a lifetime of pain to get the one thing she had a right to expect aside from her father's love and approval. Not getting those had sharpened her craving to get the ranch, to get at least one thing she had a moral right to. Ford Harlow had managed to get it for her and according to the deal, she owed him a marriage.

Her voice was little more than a whisper. ''Four days is enough.''

The glimmer in Ford's eyes flared stronger before

he looked back at her father. Rena suddenly couldn't bear another moment in the room, particularly when Ford showed no sign that he was leaving soon. It relieved her that neither man remarked or called her back when she quietly walked out.

Rena found her father's housekeeper, Myra, and told her goodbye before she headed down to the stable for her horses. She should be thrilled to inherit Lambert Ranch, but the thrill was dampened by her terror of marrying Ford.

Besides, there was always the chance her father would change his mind. She didn't trust his sudden capitulation. By tomorrow—or even later today—he could change his mind and the deal would be canceled.

And even if he didn't cancel the deal right away, there was no way to be certain her father would keep his word about Lambert Ranch indefinitely. Abner was in reasonably good health for a man his age, so it could be years before he passed away. That gave him years to find a way to thwart any legal document Ford tried to hold him to.

Until her father either passed away or reneged on the deal, Rena would be married to Ford. She didn't delude herself into thinking that this marriage was the forever kind, whatever happened with her father. They'd made a deal for land. Ford would have his right away, but it was completely possible that Abner would somehow prevent her from ever receiving hers.

The whole thing could end up in the courts, and Rena's personal assets were not enough for a prolonged fight. And a court fight would as much as advertise the fact that she and Ford had married for land. Besides, Ford would have long ago got what he wanted, so why would he bother with that kind of trouble?

Whatever happened between now and then, she'd have a marriage and she'd be a wife. What kind of marriage would it be now that Ford seemed to have effectively negotiated away her father's specific requirement for a male heir? Without the need for a son to ensure that Lambert Ranch was passed down to blood family, would Ford be interested in having children with her?

She wasn't even certain she wanted children, at least not unless having them was evidence of a solid marriage with everything a solid marriage meant, particularly love. Perhaps Ford felt the same way and he'd subtly negotiated a male heir out of the agreement because he had no desire to have children tie him to a woman he couldn't love.

And what if he'd negotiated so boldly with her father because he expected a marriage to her wouldn't last long? Abner was seventy-five and a marriage need last only until the will was read.

When she reached the stable, Frank Casey, his two sons and several of the men waited. Frank and his sons had gathered her tack and collected her horses. Frank had hooked up the horse trailer he was loaning to her, but most of them knew nothing more than the fact that she was leaving Lambert Ranch.

They hadn't loaded her two horses and the yearling filly that belonged to her, but the well-cared-for animals were tethered nearby. It surprised her a bit when all the men politely removed their hats in a rare show of formality. Frank spoke when she reached them.

"We're all sorry your leavin', Miz Lambert. Not sure how many'll care to stay on after you go."

Rena had privately informed Frank that her father had mentioned willing the ranch to him and his sons. She'd decided it was fair to let him know because if it actually was her father's plan to will Frank the ranch, Frank could spoil that for himself and his sons by quitting as foreman. Frank had rejected the notion, and it was clear he'd disapproved of her father cutting her out of her rightful inheritance.

She nodded. "I trust your judgment about whatever you and the others decide, Frank, but I need to do this."

Frank nodded solemnly and she shook his hand. His sons were next, then the men. All were somber.

She briefly exchanged good-luck wishes with each of them as Frank loaded her horses.

Rena had got along well with everyone on Lambert Ranch, but her father had always resented any sign that the men felt strong loyalty to her. The more surly and difficult Abner had become, the more the men had looked to her for decisions, though he never suspected how often that happened. Between her and the men, Lambert Ranch had managed to run reasonably well, in spite of Abner's irrational decrees.

Rena wouldn't tell anyone about the possibility that she might be marrying Ford Harlow because, besides feeling embarrassed about the circumstances, she couldn't truly believe she'd actually marry Ford. She'd lived her whole life with this kind of uncertainty, and she'd hated that, but it was always best to keep expectations for good low. Though in this case, it was hard to know which outcomes were good and which ones weren't.

Several of the men had either returned to the headquarters or stayed nearby after word had gotten around that she was leaving, so once they'd bid her a proper goodbye, they started back to work.

Rena got into her pickup and started it to drive to the front of the main house, debating where to go. She could stable her horses and check into a motel until she knew the details of Ford's deal with her father. What she truly wanted now was to forget it all and drive to Austin to begin the search for work, but the possibility of inheriting Lambert made that impossible.

Ford was just coming out of the house when she pulled to a stop next to his parked truck. He walked directly to her.

"I've already made arrangements for your horses at Harlow," he told her. "My housekeeper's got your room ready by now."

The idea that he expected her to move directly into his home increased her unease.

"I'm not sure that's a good idea," she said quietly.

The faint smile on Ford's mouth smoothed to a serious line. "Abner's antsy about you leaving Lambert. He'll focus better on keeping his end of the deal if it looks like you and I are keeping our end."

Rena glanced away and gripped the steering wheel. "And once you and I are under the same roof and people hear about it, he could back out of the agreement."

"Why would he do that?"

It was difficult to admit to Ford, but she made herself look at him to say it. "To cause…embarrassment."

Ford appeared unfazed by that. "He already knows that once you and I are together, I won't tolerate that. You seem to be the only one in doubt."

She felt a pinprick of anger but kept her voice calm. ''And you seem to be the only one who doesn't understand how my father is.''

''Sure I do. He's bad-tempered and he's a bully. Once you're away from him, he won't seem so powerful and you can stop letting him worry you.''

The words were blunt and left no room for her to mistake either Ford's opinion of her father or his disapproval of her worries.

''It's getting late,'' he went on. ''Miz Zelly had supper started before I came over, and I've worked up a hell of an appetite.''

His dark gaze held hers for long moments and she sensed a double meaning in those last words, a sexual meaning that somehow pierced her ignorance and sent a flush over her skin. Her gaze jerked from his.

''So your men and your housekeeper know about…this?'' She couldn't bring herself to call it a marriage. ''They think—''

''They think I've finally decided to marry. The shenanigans of a bitter old man, whatever those might be, won't influence what they'll think of you.''

This was his second dismissal of her worries about what her father might do. Frustrated by that, she was compelled to convince him her worries weren't groundless.

''The man's reputation doesn't suffer what a

woman's does." She glanced at him in time to catch the start of his smile.

Ford leaned toward the truck to rest a forearm on the sill of the open window. Which brought his face disturbingly close to hers. His voice dropped lower, and his words sent a double stroke of heat through her.

"Civilized people used to marry each other to stop wagging tongues. We can do that if the land deal falls through and you're still worried about how this looks."

Rena felt again that peculiar mix of fear and excitement, but she couldn't seem to pull her gaze away.

"We need to get moving," he said then. "It'd be nice to have you settled in before supper. We've got plans to work out before we get the license tomorrow."

Her insides were quivering with added anxiety at the mention of a marriage license, but she did her best to conceal it. Besides, she hadn't yet thanked Ford for what he'd accomplished for her. She made an awkward start.

"I'm obliged to you for putting yourself out in there with my father, and I'm...grateful."

He came right back with, "We're both obliged. To each other for what we'll get out of the deal, and for a marriage."

There it was again, that glimpse of implacability. The fear Rena felt made her give a nod before she faced forward, relieved when Ford turned to walk to his truck.

The moment his back was turned, she secretly watched him go, wondering how on earth she would ever adjust to him.

Ford had seen the fear in Rena's troubled gaze. She was terrified of marrying him. He'd be willing to bet her terror was sharp enough that she'd almost give up the chance to inherit Lambert Ranch if it meant she wouldn't have to go through with a wedding.

He wasn't offended by that, he was touched. Unfortunately there might be little he could do to ease her terror in the short time between now and the end of the week.

Perhaps it wasn't fair to try. Her father had put her in an impossible position, and Ford himself had just upped the ante for her. To be honest, he didn't trust Abner any more than she did, but the details of the legal agreement he'd be signing might at least make the old man think twice about reneging later.

In the meantime, he had to somehow keep Rena from bolting while he tried to decide if getting his hands on more land and water was truly worth the trouble of marrying her.

*   *   *

By the time Rena angled the horse trailer near the stable at Harlow Ranch, she was shaking. She switched off the truck engine and got out to unload her horses, sick with misgiving.

Ford had driven in ahead of her and now he joined her to open the trailer gate and pull out the ramp. He introduced three of his ranch hands who offered to take care of her horses, but Rena gently declined, preferring to settle them in herself.

"Then one of you can get this trailer unhitched and taken back to Frank Casey at Lambert Ranch," Ford told his men as he took the two horses' lead ropes, leaving the filly for Rena. "The other two can take her truck up to the house. Miz Zelly'll show you where to put Miz Lambert's things."

Rena got in a quiet "Thank you" to the men, though Ford's brisk directions to them cranked her nerves several notches higher. Things were happening too fast. She should have been able to slow them down, to reconsider the shocking events of the day and make certain what she truly wanted, but her brain was pounding with it all.

The filly immediately began to act up, yanking away and fidgeting at the end of her lead. The abrupt move claimed Rena's attention and she struggled to calm herself while she gave the filly a reassuring rub. Ford had already taken her horses into the stable, so Rena led the filly and followed.

Three large stalls halfway down had been prepared, complete with measures of grain and fresh water. Rena put the filly in the center stall, removed her
halter, then waited while the yearling inspected her
new quarters. Her horses took the change in stride.
Ford and the ranch hand who was returning the
trailer to Frank Casey got her tack stowed in the tack
room, and once Rena was satisfied her animals were
comfortable, she joined Ford for the walk to the main
house.

The Harlow Ranch house was a sprawling two-
story Victorian, with a large back patio overhung by
leafy shade trees. Both the front and back verandas
were decorated with urns of colorful flowers, which
gave the whole place a look of energy and hospital-
ity.

Nothing like the stark simplicity of the Lambert
Ranch house, which had always seemed colorless
and grim.

The kitchen was alive with the same vitality and
color, from the display of hanging cookware over a
large island counter in the main part, to the hanging
pots of flowers and trailing vines and gaily colored
tile of the large floor.

Food preparations were scattered over the island
counter and parts of two others. The warm smell of
baking bread and the rich aroma of roasting beef reminded Rena she hadn't eaten since breakfast.

Zelly Norman turned from her work to give them a wide smile of welcome. Ford quickly introduced her to Rena, who greeted the small woman quietly.

"She's a handsome choice, Boss," Zelly remarked, and Rena was uneasy with the expression.

She considered the word handsome a masculine word, or one related to horses, but the happy smile on Zelly's face couldn't be mistaken for anything less than genuine approval and enthusiasm.

"Welcome to Harlow Ranch," Zelly went on. "I hope you're happy here. Let me know if there's anything you need."

"Thank you," Rena said, unable to defeat the awkwardness she felt or the tremor of her smile.

Ford whisked her away for a quick tour of his home. The house was far larger than the Lambert main house, the rooms spacious and filled with light. The dimness and hint of oppression she was accustomed to was absent here.

It was a man's house, with lots of wood and leather and color, but the feminine touches—needlework pillows, the occasional delicate chair or watercolor painting and burst of ruffled curtains—made it all a pleasing combination that interested the eye, and Rena was surprisingly comfortable with the homey feel of it.

The upstairs tour dampened that feeling of comfort, if for no other reason than the fact that she'd never been near a bedroom in a man's presence, much less accompanied a man into his own bedroom.

She might have lingered outside the room if she'd realized the huge bedroom was Ford's, but he'd led her past most of the other six doors along the hall to this one, so she'd assumed he was leading her directly to the room his housekeeper had prepared for her.

The masculinity of the room and the obvious absence of her boxes of belongings, made her halt uncertainly a few feet inside.

"This'll be our room after the ceremony on Friday. The walk-in's big enough for your things, so we can move in all but what you need every day as soon as you want to unpack. Zelly's cleared drawers in the dresser and the chest in here for what you don't want in the closet. Your room's through there," he said, indicating the door at the side of the room, "to make it convenient."

Rena's startled gaze shot toward the open door that connected Ford's bedroom with the next one. Ford went on as if he'd sensed the spark of horror she felt and meant to confront it head-on.

"We'll be sharing a bed in a handful of days. It's best for us to live close to each other's habits between now and then."

"I won't sleep with you."

The quiet words came out on a whispery gust. Ford's response to that was instant.

"And I won't marry a woman I can't share a bed with. You need to plan on that." The soft declaration made her heart fall, then kick into a wild beat. She looked at him, dismayed that his expression was hard and no-nonsense.

"There's n-no need for a son."

"Not for you to inherit, but I want sons," he went on. "And daughters. I won't marry a woman who's not willing to bear my children."

He was so brutally candid that she felt the room shift. "What if we're not...suited?"

His stern expression didn't ease. "Then we'd better set our minds on *suiting* each other before we go through a ceremony on Friday."

Though his voice was still low and calm, its steely undertone wrapped around her and squeezed mercilessly. The urge to escape him was profound, but she managed to stifle it.

"What if I...change my mind about this? Or you do?"

Ford's gaze searched hers. "Then I reckon there'll be no marriage."

His words only marginally eased the terrified thundering of her heart. Was the possibility of inheriting Lambert Ranch truly worth all this? If Ford was anything like her father, she'd be trading one tyrant for another. Only this tyrant, Ford, was the one who was the most potentially dangerous.

She'd had no choice about how she'd grown up. She'd be choosing to marry Ford, whatever the incentive, so that meant she'd be getting everything good or bad that would come with that choice.

What kind of man was he, truly?

"You ought to have a look at your room," he said, and she realized she must have stared at him all this time. And, because he seemed so unerringly perceptive, he'd probably at least glimpsed evidence of her chaotic thoughts.

This man was too strong for her. Worldly, *experienced* Ford Harlow, who seemed to detect everything, could make mincemeat of her heart and scatter it in the dust without a backward glance.

She jerked her gaze from his face and walked stiffly to the connecting door for the expected glance into the room Ford had assigned her. The details—beyond the orderly stacks of boxes near the connecting door—made absolutely no impression on her. Her whole being seemed only able to focus on the man who stood behind her and the questions that whirled in her brain.

"We need to wash up for supper. Zelly serves at six."

Ford's voice was quiet, as if he'd sensed it all, as if he'd known that she was scrambling for something normal to fix on, for something to distract her from the pressure of the shocking demands he'd detailed to her.

All over a piece of land and an inheritance. The notion of marrying a stranger to get either seemed both foreign and immoral. To be expected to sleep with a man she didn't know from the first day of that marriage was barbaric.

And, for a woman who'd never been kissed, who'd never so much as held a man's hand, it was absolutely horrifying.

Somehow, she turned and managed to walk out of Ford's bedroom into the hall, her heart beating so wildly that she was light-headed.

CHAPTER THREE

SUPPER was somber and quiet. The silence in the big dining room was measured by the heavy *tock-tock* of the ancient grandfather clock at the side of the room. Ford sat at the head of the long table, with Rena to his right.

The polished surface of the glossy dark wood reflected the soft lights of the ornate candelabra that had been placed near their end of the long table. A bowl of cut flowers sat at the base of the candelabra.

The look, as Zelly must have intended, was romantic, right down to the delicate china she'd laid out and the champagne Ford had poured and toasted them with. They both still wore their work clothes from that day, and the odd mix of romantic refinements and common clothes seemed symbolic of a marriage made for ranch land.

Except that no true romance existed beyond the candles, the flowers and champagne. The sight was a startling depiction of the truth: their marriage agreement was focused almost entirely on land, and the only romance in the deal amounted to table decorations put there by a well-meaning third party.

The food was excellent, and Rena got more of it

down than she'd expected, but she felt self-conscious every moment. It was a huge relief when they finished and Ford suggested they take their champagne to the chairs on the front veranda.

Ford waited until she'd chosen a seat, then dragged one of the other chairs closer to hers and sat down. He'd angled his chair so they faced each other a bit. Rena took a sip of the champagne she still had left, but was too tense to relax.

"We're gonna need to talk to each other, Rena. I enjoy the sound of your voice and I'd be interested in anything you'd have to say."

Rena glanced toward him, startled. *I enjoy the sound of your voice.* Sweetness trickled through her but she had no clue how to respond to what he'd said. Maybe his compliment wasn't true, but the element of kindness in his invitation to talk increased her frustration with herself.

"I'm not good at small talk," she said at last.

"It'll get easier as we go along." Ford leaned back in his chair as if he were settling in for the evening.

"I don't want to be this...uncomfortable."

"Me, neither. So how 'bout we skip to talk we'd both naturally have things to say about?"

Her soft, "Fine," was anything but the truth.

The serious issues between them were no less intimidating for her than making small talk, but there were several things they needed to discuss, and soon.

The time between now and Friday was short. So short that she almost wished her father would change his mind.

"I reckon it's been a shocking day for you."

Rena nodded and briefly pulled her gaze from the quiet probe of his.

"Did I sound cold-blooded upstairs?"

The question surprised her and she gave him an immediate "Yes," then looked over at him. She didn't add that she'd also thought he'd been domineering.

"You gonna back out of the deal?"

Her gaze shied from his calm study. "It's probably best to let this all go." Rena came to her feet in a burst of restlessness and set her champagne flute on a nearby table to walk to the veranda rail and stare out over the front lawn.

Ford's voice was calm, but it carried a hard edge. "I want that land. You want Lambert Ranch. *Can* you just let it go?"

Rena took a steadying breath. "Everybody loses something they want," she said quietly.

"Except in this case, you'd be choosing to lose Lambert Ranch."

Hearing him say it that way increased her pain. "It's not a clear choice between getting land or not getting it."

And it wasn't. Inheriting Lambert was her moral

right, but her father had put a very dangerous stipulation on it. One that virtually guaranteed a devastating emotional outcome for her, particularly if he also found a way to marry her off then backed out of his part of the deal later.

"You've put up with a lot to stay on with Abner so you could eventually get what's rightfully yours," Ford said as if he'd read her mind. "And now it looks like you've got another few years to endure in a marriage to me."

Ford's low voice carried no trace of anger or even a hint that he was offended by that. He'd made it sound like a simple and logical observation. Nevertheless, she felt compelled to apologize.

"I mean you no personal offense."

"None taken," he said mildly. "But maybe I should tell you what I have in mind. It'll either make you feel better about this or run you off completely."

Rena turned to face him and he leaned forward to rest his forearms on his thighs. Rena eased back against the veranda rail, as much to brace herself as to give the false impression that she was relaxed.

"I know this is a business deal," he began, his rugged face utterly somber. "Others will know it, too, but there's a marriage involved and I think you and I need to give the marriage part a fair effort."

He was working up to another sleeping-in-the-same-bed-and-having-children discussion or, as he'd

told her that morning, convenient sex and having
kids.

"Y-you already said that. Sleeping together and
having children," she said, then felt heat go up her
cheeks to her hairline. She felt impossibly backward
and glanced away. It was a moment before she could
find the nerve to look over at him again. And a moment more before he answered.

"I want those things and more, Rena. Much
more." His voice had gone a bit lower, and the heat
she felt in her face went over her whole body to her
toes. "That means I'd like us to be a bride and
groom. To take the husband and wife part seriously."

She had no response to that. Partly because she
couldn't think of anything to say, partly because she
sensed he meant to say more.

"That means my focus is on you and yours is on
me. As if this was an ordinary marriage."

Rena found it difficult to get in a normal breath.
An ordinary marriage. As if he truly wanted something more with her than sex and children in a love-
less bargain to get land. The secret attraction she'd
felt toward him in the past—the attraction that had
all but been frightened away that day—suddenly began to quiver and rise.

"I'd like to see you in a pretty dress Friday," he
went on in that same low, gravelly voice. "You don't
have to wear something satiny that drags the floor

unless you want to. And if you want to, I'd like to do this in a church with a preacher instead of in front of a judge at the courthouse. I'd like to have other people there to witness it.''

His mention of a satin dress, a church and other people sent a fresh spear of dread through her. She hadn't had time to consider how public a life she might have to live if she married Ford Harlow.

And it promised to be a very public life. Her father was an elderly crank who'd kept mostly to himself and insisted she do the same, but Ford was well-known and he constantly interacted with people in the local town and ranching community. He was very high profile in their part of Texas, so any woman he married would have the same high profile visibility.

And Rena was what she was, a mannish female with only basic social graces, too reserved and socially inexperienced to feel comfortable or confident. She had no idea how much it was possible to learn, and what if she didn't catch on fast enough? She could easily cause them both dozens of social embarrassments.

''I'm doing all the talking, Rena, and I don't think you want that.'' He smiled gently. ''You'll learn right off that if you don't speak up, I'll tend to take over.''

''I'm not sure I want…that much,'' she said quietly.

"And I want everything," he countered.

Rena felt the peculiar pleasure-fear, but it seemed to gather and pool in every feminine part of her and grow warm.

"We're strangers," she told him, not able yet to confess her worries about living with him or her fears about embarrassing them both and disappointing him. Or worse, earning his animosity.

"And we might not suit each other," he said, re-minding her of what she'd told him earlier.

"Yes."

The silence stretched out for long, long moments.

"So how do you think we should go about finding out whether we suit each other?"

His soft question was a concession to her worries about that, but it also pressured her to give him an answer. She'd been wary of his dominance earlier, but he wasn't dominating her now, at least he wasn't issuing a series of declarations as he had in his bed-room earlier. His ongoing silence—his *waiting* si-lence—gave the strong impression that he could wait all evening for her to give him an answer.

And what should she say, what *could* she say? She didn't really know how men and women truly got to know each other, because she'd never seen it close up. Honesty made her prone to telling him the truth about herself and that was another little terror. But Ford was perceptive and he was worldly. Most of all, he was experienced and he made his way in life confidently and successfully. She'd probably lose nothing but another bit of her pride if she was completely honest. She wouldn't be telling him anything he couldn't have already guessed.

"I'm not…very experienced with men," she began shakily and felt her courage waver. "Not in the way you want to talk about." She looked away from him briefly because his calm gaze seemed to go straight into her brain. But this next was too important not to try to see how he reacted, so she forced herself to look at him.

"I know I don't want to be bullied and I don't want to be run over and bossed. I don't want to be made a fool of."

She swallowed hard and tried to get the rest out. "And I don't want to make you look foolish when I make mistakes while we'd be married. That's why I think it's best for both of us to just let this all go. Once I'm out of the way, my father will sell you the land. Or lease it to you. I'll let him know it was me who stopped the deal. He'll believe it, and you'll be clear."

"Can you look me in the eye and tell me you aren't at least a little curious about what being married to me might be like?"

There it was, a hint that he'd seen her interest in him and had somehow figured out she had a crush on him. He'd ignored her worry about making mistakes, and instead targeted this. It made her wary of him and her instinct was to try to counter his perception.

"It's best to not entertain such thoughts," she said awkwardly. She couldn't help the hot color that went over her face. Ford's dark eyes seemed to note that, but he continued on.

"You're a poor liar, Rena."

The gentle remark was so accurate that she felt ashamed to have tried to evade him. The best she could do then was turn his question back on him. "Can you tell me you honestly think you'd be happy or satisfied with a woman like me?" she dared softly. "I'm sure you could take your pick of others."

"Maybe. I want a woman who loves ranch life as much as I do. The fact that the one I'm looking at seems to and is also beautiful and appealing to me is a bonus I'm satisfied with."

Rena had to look away then as cynicism and pleasure warred in her heart. He said so many right things. The words came easily to him and sounded wonderful to a woman who'd heard too few nice things.

She was bright enough to realize that Ford Harlow could easily mesmerize her with false flattery. He could probably mesmerize a woman like her in any way he chose if he made even the smallest effort.

And he'd somehow said it all with a straight face and with a somber look in his dark eyes that seemed completely sincere.

And still was when she looked his way again in time for him to say, "You don't believe me."

She told him the truth. "How can I be sure you wouldn't say all this just to get that land? You know as well as I do that you could fool me."

One corner of Ford's stern mouth quirked up in a half smile. "You're too damned suspicious to be fooled, Rena. I'll have a hard road with you just to earn your trust."

"Why bother? As I sa—"

"Because we're both after something we want," he cut in, "so we're on the same side. Marriage usually cements a relationship at the end of courtship, but ours will come at the beginning. Or almost the beginning, since we've got four days before the ceremony. And no, I wouldn't say just anything to a woman to get a piece of land. If the woman didn't already appeal to me, no amount of land would ever be enough to change my mind."

The sudden silence between them seemed to expand and bear down heavily on her. She felt the pressure of Ford's expectation and her gaze fled his.

It warmed her to know she appealed to him. He wasn't known as a liar, though the word "appeal" only meant so much.

But he'd stood up to her father on her behalf and she couldn't forget that. Or the fact that it obligated her. And what he wanted from her—what he clearly expected—was that she'd fall into line with his agreement with her father and go through with the wedding.

But Ford had other expectations, and those were the ones that worried her most.

Convenient sex and children…those things and more…an ordinary marriage…

Expectations that other women would consider wonderful, but to her were fraught with enormous risk.

But what about the secret crush she'd had on him all this time? The crush she still had? Hadn't her naive daydreams of somehow attracting his notice and perhaps even winning some level of his approval held at least the magic seed of hope for love and marriage and family?

It surprised her now to realize that her heart had never seriously entertained a craving for marriage and family because she'd thought that was too much to hope for, too painful to let herself want when she doubted she could ever have either one.

And yet here she was on the verge of marrying Ford Harlow, who'd made it clear he wanted children with her. Maybe she could have a real family and a place in one that, whatever the difficulties, could never be as barren and lonely and harsh as the life she'd lived up to now.

But the potential for disaster with Ford countered that bit of wishful thinking. She'd never survive it if he ever developed the same devastating enmity toward her that her father had.

Because she'd taken so long to respond to Ford's unspoken question and the heavy crush of silence and indecision was still pressing her, she gave a faint start when Ford spoke.

"You said you don't want to be bullied or bossed or made a fool of. You need to hear from me that I wouldn't bully or make a fool of you. And the world won't explode in a fireball if you stand up to me when I get bossy."

Now she looked at him again, searching his rugged face to gauge his sincerity.

"Will you marry me, Rena, and give this an honest try?"

Rena struggled to remind herself that Ford wanted the land, but she couldn't help the pleasure that flooded her because he'd formally proposed. And though the potential for hurt was far greater than the potential for good, she realized that in the end, she felt too obligated to him to turn him down.

Her soft, "Yes," was barely audible and she trembled with the fear that came next.

She'd just, in essence, either opened herself for the

most devastating hurt of her life or the most wonderful blessing.

"I'd like to check on my horses," she got out,
suddenly desperate to escape him and find some bit
of privacy to think about what she'd done. The in-
appropriateness of bluntly mentioning her horses immediately after accepting Ford's marriage proposal
sent a stroke of mortification through her, but Ford
accepted the abrupt change of subject as if it'd been
the natural next thing to say.

"I haven't shown you around yet, so we could do
that after."

Rena's hope for privacy would have to wait, and
maybe it had to. If she was truly going to marry Ford
on Friday, the most important thing was to get used
to him.

But as they started for the stable, the touch of his
hand on her arm set off a cascade of sensation and
she had to struggle to conceal any sign of the pleasure she felt.

That next day was a marathon of shopping once
they'd applied for the marriage license. They'd gone
to San Antonio, and Rena had separated from Ford
to frantically shop for everything from basic makeup
to wedding clothes.

She'd needed to be tutored to apply the makeup,
and it was certain she'd need to practice in private

before she'd be able to get all the recommended steps and applications right on her own. She was pleased with the result and caught herself glancing in windows and mirrors wherever she went to remind herself that the difference was just as thrilling as when she'd first had a look.

Because she owned no truly feminine clothes, she found herself trying on and buying several things that caught her eye. She'd accumulated a surprising number of shopping bags before she let herself face the fact that she'd been delaying the choice of what to select for the ceremony on Friday.

Ford caught up with her by then and relieved her of the bags to take them to his car. His parting reminder about the nearby bridal shop prompted her to finally go directly to it.

Once inside, her plaid shirt, jeans and boots seemed distinctly out of place. When she caught a glimpse of herself in another mirror and against the backdrop of white froth and lace, she realized she looked like a made-up country hick too masculine to be a bride.

A little heartsick, she was about to slip out of the shop and perhaps come back the next day wearing some of her new, more feminine clothes, when one of the shop clerks intercepted her.

Too polite and uncertain to decline the woman's

offer to wait on her, Rena answered her initial questions.

"Friday? Well, honey, we don't have a minute to waste!" the clerk declared, and Rena found herself going on a tour of the shop as the clerk showed her a number of beautiful gowns.

The woman hadn't seemed to care about her jeans and boots so Rena felt herself relax. Though on the drive to San Antonio Ford had repeated his preference for a wedding dress and a church ceremony, then mentioned it again before he'd taken her things to the car, Rena rejected the notion of an elaborate dress with a train.

She gently declined the first few gowns the clerk presented and, after a little more questioning, she led Rena to another tall rack.

The floor-length gown she showed Rena then was the first one that truly appealed to her. The long-sleeved gown was white satin, with a light spangle of seed pearls across the low-cut fitted bodice that was highlighted by a modest garden of shiny white embroidered flowers with more seed pearls. The veil was a froth of delicate netting, with more seed pearls on the wide comb that would anchor the veil. It was hardly as simple as she'd meant to find, but it had an old-fashioned feminine elegance that she found hard to resist.

The clerk helped her collect the proper foundation

garments to go with the gown, then rushed her into one of the large changing rooms. Despite Rena's acute embarrassment, the woman helped her change.

The gown was a perfect fit and Rena stared into the mirrors that showed her the look from every angle. The gown was beautiful.

"Oh my, honey," the clerk said with quiet enthusiasm, "that's the one for you."

So far, Rena had only looked at the gown. Now she dared a look at her face, and the combination of makeup and the magic of the dress made her look utterly feminine. She dropped her gaze back down to the gown's reflection as the clerk went on.

"You'll have to get your hair styled different later, but we should fit you with shoes right away."

The clerk had no more than said that and asked for her size before she ducked out and went on a search. Rena again looked at herself in the mirror. This time, she felt better about the bride—the almost beautiful bride—who stared steadily back.

However certain the clerk was that the gown was perfect for her, Rena stepped outside the bridal shop to find Ford before she wrote out the check. She didn't want to buy a dress that didn't fit what he had in mind for the ceremony.

She'd never been to a wedding herself, and though she'd fallen utterly in love with the gown that seemed to be the zenith of femininity, she would be devastated if she bought it then found out Ford disapproved.

A little ashamed to be so uncertain about her choice, it was nevertheless a fact that her femininity had been so stunted by relentless criticism that she had little confidence in her instincts. And she would rigidly avoid any situation that might cause Ford to make a negative comment on her lack as a woman, so it made sense to her that it would be better to have him make his comments now, while there was still time to make another selection.

When she found him, Ford cut off the conversation he'd been having on his cell phone to give her his full attention, then walked through the mall with her to the bridal shop.

"Isn't it supposed to be bad luck for the groom to see the dress before the ceremony?" he asked as they walked into the shop.

Rena halted and sent him a quick glance. "Bad luck?"

"Yes." Ford smiled. "Bad luck to see the bride's dress, bad luck for the bride and groom to see each other before the ceremony on the day of the wedding. All those 'something old, something new, something borrowed, something blue' superstitions."

Anxiety quivered to life. "You're superstitious?"

Ford's smile widened and something in her re-laxed a little. "No. Are you?"

"I don't think so."

"Good. Because bad luck is the last thing you and I need to bother with. Let's have a look at that dress."

Relief smoothed away some of her anxiety. "Will you tell me if you think it's...too much?"

"It won't be too much," he scoffed gently, and Rena felt a soft burst of gratitude and affection for him. The kindness she'd seen in him before—the kindness that had caused her secret feelings for him to blossom years ago—made a fresh impact on her emotions.

She led the way to the rack by the cash register to show him the gown that hung there.

Ford obligingly looked at it and nervousness made her give him a shaky, "I meant to find a simpler dress, so I still can if you don't mind another wait. M-maybe if you look around and point out—"

"Perfect."

"—something...better," she finished belatedly, mortified by her nervous babble and the stark inse-curity she'd just paraded in front of him.

"Perfect." The repeated pronouncement was firm and left no room for doubt.

Relief went over her like a calming wave until she saw him reach for his wallet. She put out a hand, but stopped just short of actually touching him. His dark gaze met hers and she could tell he'd noticed.

"I'll be out in a minute," she said, knowing he'd take it as she meant it: that she would pay for her own gown.

Nevertheless, when he left her to settle the bill, her hand shook as she wrote out the check. Whether her father stuck to the deal and they went through with the ceremony, or he changed his mind and it was canceled, she was buying a very costly dress.

For a woman who'd rarely bought anything other than work clothes, it was a momentous event. And for a woman who'd never owned anything so completely beautiful and feminine, it was a milestone.

CHAPTER FOUR

BY THE time they got back to Harlow Ranch, Rena was in a kind of shock. When everything she'd bought that day was hung in her closet, she lingered in her room for a few minutes of privacy to recover.

The diamond engagement ring on her left hand seemed extravagant. She'd never worn a ring, but even if she had, this one would have taken getting used to.

The ring was gorgeous, but the weight of obligation she felt about going through with the ceremony and a marriage made it feel as if it weighted five pounds.

Ford had already preselected several rings at one of the most exclusive jewelers in San Antonio. There had been nothing on the velvet ring tray to disclose prices, but a surreptitious glance around at the price of other pieces had let her know that the rings Ford had meant for her to choose from were outlandishly expensive.

When she'd privately asked him if the rings could be returned if the wedding fell through, he'd ignored the question, instead prompting her to try them all on before she made her choice.

Aware that Ford might have firm ideas about what he'd want his wife to wear, she'd ended up declining a choice. Ford had promptly selected the most elaborate—and probably the most expensive—set of rings.

Her mental review of the day underscored how far out of her element she was and how awkwardly she'd dealt with it all. She felt like a country hick and today she must have seemed every ounce a hick to Ford. Had his approval of her gown and his choice of the elaborate ring set been an effort to feminize his mannish bride-to-be? She could hardly be offended by that because everything she'd bought for herself that day had been her own attempt to feminize herself.

Through it all, Ford had been patience and kindness personified, and she couldn't help that her feelings for him were growing. Feelings that were more risky for her than buying the costly gown and allowing Ford to buy the extravagant rings when Friday was so uncertain.

If her father changed his mind and canceled the deal, both she and Ford would either have to face the embarrassment of returning the gown and the rings, or she'd at least feel compelled to reimburse him for what he'd spent.

Her bank account had already been quite severely dented that day, so it was a realistic worry. That was why she wouldn't remove the tag from the gown until the moment she was ready to put it on for the ceremony.

Too restless to sit still, Rena began to pace. Tomorrow she'd drive to San Antonio to find a beauty shop and see about her hair. Though it looked fine to her, she'd taken seriously the remark the shop clerk had made about having it styled differently. She'd also search out a bookstore to find a book on weddings and another on etiquette.

The brief knock on the hall door was a reminder that Zelly was about to serve supper, so she went out to join Ford and go downstairs.

As if their day of shopping hadn't made her head spin, Ford's plan for them to go to a local Country Western nightclub later that evening made her dizzy with giddy anxiety. She'd never been anyplace like that, but the notion was as exciting as it was worrisome.

Ford had made it clear that he believed people needed to see them together before Friday, but that only heightened her nervousness. Grateful that she'd bought new clothes that would be suitable, she'd retreated to her room after supper to look through the closet to make a choice.

Cowardice made her leave the dresses on their hangers. Ford had told her to dress casually, and since dressing up literally meant dresses or skirts to her, she selected a simple white blouse and khaki slacks. And, for the first time in recent memory, she left her boots in favor of the pair of modest black heels she'd also bought that day. After freshening her makeup, she put a few items in the small handbag she'd bought to go with the heels.

The young woman in the mirror looked crisply dressed, but the light makeup, handbag and heels made her look more feminine and somehow softer. Surprised at the difference she saw in her image, Rena started across the bedroom to go downstairs to wait for Ford when he knocked on the connecting door.

She walked over to open it, almost relieved that he would see her now in case what she'd chosen to wear was somehow inappropriate.

Ford was dressed in jeans, but he'd selected a red-and-white striped Western shirt. He'd also shaved, and she liked the subtle scent of his spicy aftershave. She read the approval in his dark gaze and felt herself relax a little.

"Do you know how to dance?" he asked, and she felt a ripple of tension return.

"No."

"I enjoy it, so you'll probably get a lesson to-night," he said, then touched her arm to usher her out of the room and into the hall. "Nothing fancy, but you ought to expect that once we're on the dance floor, men'll want to cut in."

"That won't happen," she said with soft candor as they walked down the hall.

"Count on it like you count on the sun coming up in the morning." Ford smiled at her when she glanced doubtfully at him. "Dance with them until I can cut back in, but make sure you give that ring a little flash."

Rena faced forward and touched the ring band with her thumb, uneasy with his assumption. Before she could say so, they'd started down the stairs and he went on.

"The single men in these parts have been wondering for years when Rena Lambert will show up for something more than a trip to the feed store."

Rena's gaze swung to his. She was surprised that he would toy with her like this, but it surprised her more to realize how much his teasing disappointed her.

"You're joking with me."

"Then tonight'll be a revelation for you, Miz Rena," he said as they reached the last steps. "Just don't forget who brought you."

If anything, Ford had underestimated the response of the single men in the local community. Though it was a workday night, the nightclub was crowded. A country band played at the far end of the huge room, and the dance floor between the tables and the band was already filling up with dancers.

She and Ford found a table not too far from the dance floor and once they were seated, Ford ordered them something to drink. He settled back and Rena sat tensely as several of the other patrons began a virtual parade past their table to greet Ford and get a quick introduction to her.

After that and what Ford had said earlier, she was more alert to the interested gazes of the men and it truly was a revelation, but it was a shock when three of the cowboys had been bold enough to ask her to dance. She'd falteringly turned them down, and they'd taken it pleasantly. Ford had given her an ''I told you so'' look that prompted an edgy smile from her.

A small, curvy brunette was one of the women who came by. Rena remembered Jenny Sharpe from school. Jenny had been very popular but Rena hadn't been part of her social circle or any of the others, though no one had gone out of their way to exclude her. The circumstances of Rena's home life had made close friends impossible, so she'd focused almost completely on school work and getting good grades.

''Well, Rena Lambert!'' Jenny declared, leaning toward them and raising her voice to be heard over the sound of the band. "Haven't seen much of you since graduation. How're you doin'?"

Jenny's friendliness seemed completely genuine and Rena responded with a smile. Jenny's bright gaze dropped to Rena's left hand and she reached over to take her fingers and lift them for a closer inspection.

"My Lord, would you look at that rock? I heard you two were getting married Friday, but what will the two of you live on after buyin' this?" Jenny released Rena's hand and grinned at Ford. "The next few men around here are gonna feel it in their wallets when they have to come up with something as impressive for their sweethearts. Congratulations, Ford. Hope you'll bring your new bride to my daddy's barbecue in a couple weeks so we can all finally get to know her."

Rena felt a spark of pleasure and relief. Even she knew that an invitation from Jenny Sharpe virtually ensured acceptance. Jenny saw someone else she wanted to visit with and after giving them both her best wishes, she hurried off.

Ford touched her arm and leaned closer as the band finished one tune and then started the first notes of a Garth Brooks ballad.

"Let's dance this one. Start with something slow and simple."

He stood up and Rena did, too, though she was

nervous about this. Ford's light grip on her hand was comforting and thrilling, but when they reached the dance floor and he turned to face her, she drew back a half step before she could catch herself.

Ford was looking down at her and she saw it in his eyes when he noted her small retreat. There was something assertive about the way he gave her hand a tug to pull her closer, then slid his free hand around her waist to pull her against him.

Surprise and self-consciousness made her go stiff. They touched each other lightly from chest to knee and Rena stared blindly at the hard line of his jaw. She put up her free hand to his shoulder, but hesitated a few moments with her hand barely resting on it, uncomfortable with the embrace that felt anything but natural.

The heat from Ford's big body was scorching as was the harsh heat of modesty that burned over her face. The arm around her waist held her loosely but neither of them moved. Ford's voice was a husky rasp.

"Goin' too fast for you?" His warm breath tickled her eyelashes.

"We haven't started yet," she said.

"You're gonna do fine. Relax, look at the other dancers and move with me."

Ford started and the steps were slow and simple enough for her to easily keep track. It took her a moment to register that the male heat of his body was literally melting the stiffness from hers. She couldn't seem to help that each move they made caused her to sink a little more firmly against him.

Her body had somehow gone feverish in every feminine spot, and the pleasure-fear Ford had always stirred set off an odd craving inside that she understood as purely sexual. Her mind flinched from the notion, but her body responded and what she'd first thought was fear was actually a restless kind of excitement.

Just then Ford passed her off to one of the men who'd come by their table earlier. It was as if her body had been rudely jolted out of a languor of pleasure, and though she felt herself go rigid with self-consciousness, being in the cowboy's arms was far less sexually personal than it had been with Ford.

Rena managed to hold herself a hand span from the cowboy and it was immediately clear that he was a graceless dancer, though he also seemed happily enthusiastic about it. She barely managed to keep from being stepped on before one of the other men cut in and she was again passed off.

The remarkable difference was that neither of her two partners—and then a third—provoked even a faint hint of what she'd felt in Ford's arms. Though the third one silently demanded closer dancing than the first two when his arm tightened snuggly around her waist, the most she felt was annoyance. Ford quickly cut back in and the restless excitement she'd felt only with him surged back.

The next dance was a lively two-step which she followed awkwardly at first, then caught on to. Other partners were frequent, but she truly enjoyed the faster paced, arm's length dances.

When Ford finally led her back to their table, she was surprisingly happy. She'd not made a fool of herself and the large crowd now seemed far less intimidating. The acceptance she'd yearned for her whole life had been granted, and by the time they walked out of the nightclub later, Rena felt a warm glow of confidence.

The ride back to Harlow Ranch was quiet and swift, but when they'd got there and gone upstairs, Ford walked into her room with her and caught her hand. Just that quickly, he pulled her close and his big hands gently gripped her waist. She lifted her hands reflexively and her palms now rested lightly on his chest.

He was looking down at her, the glimmer in his gaze evidence that he was watching her alertly.

"You liked it tonight, didn't you." It was more an assessment than a serious question.

Worry touched her then. Her father would have found fault with any sign that she'd enjoyed herself. And though Ford didn't appear to be like that, she had danced with other men. He'd expected that, but would he criticize her for appearing to have a good time with anyone besides him? For her, it was a realistic worry.

"I didn't forget who took me to the dance," she said uneasily to remind him what he'd told her before they'd left for the nightclub.

The glimmer in his eyes flared and his gaze narrowed on her face. "You're worried. Why?"

She wasn't daring enough to give him a truthful answer, but she didn't want to lie. Her brain scrambled for an answer, then hit on something that was just as true a worry as dancing with other men and having a good time.

"We're h-here," she said quietly. "It's late and we're…like this. In a bedroom."

"We're engaged," he pointed out, but the probing gleam of his gaze didn't relent. As if he knew she was evading him and hadn't yet decided whether to let her get by with it. "Will you be scandalized if I kiss you?"

Rena's tension yanked tight. She'd never kissed anyone, and though she'd known marrying Ford made kisses inevitable, she'd not thought those would start soon.

Ford's voice was low and held a gentle undertone of amusement. "If you were a horse, I'd say you were about to bolt. Or at least shy away."

Rena felt her face go hot. He'd got it exactly right. And now she was virtually bracing her palms against his chest to keep him a safe distance and was helpless to keep from doing so.

Tonight had been a boost to her self-esteem, but she wasn't confident at all about passing some unknown criteria for a lover's kiss. She wasn't even able to order her thoughts enough now to search for what she thought a first kiss might be like or how it should happen.

For the past two days she'd been too overwhelmed and rushed to torture herself further by speculating about the traumatizing details and intimate mechanics of such things as kissing, sharing a bed or having children.

And Ford was probably too experienced to be satisfied with a woman who wasn't good at kissing and sex. Even with her limited understanding of men, she knew good sex was as high a priority for them as frequency was supposed to be.

"You're obviously thinking virginal thoughts, Rena," he said, but his voice had gone even lower and sounded amazingly raspy and unsteady. The glimmer in his dark eyes had turned utterly serious, and now an intensity blazed there that let her know he was about to have his way. "Don't you want to know before Friday?"

Panicked, Rena dropped her gaze to his shirtfront. Ford's fingers flexed warmly on her waist.

"You have such a pretty mouth," he said, his voice a gruff whisper. "It looks tender and soft, but there's something about it that I always thought said, 'Go slow.'"

And the way he was easing closer was also slow. Rena's gaze slid up to his, then back down. Her eyelashes fluttered as his warm breath feathered against them. The pleasure-fear sent such a weakness through her that she was certain the sensation was mostly fear. But then a heavy warmth began to pulse in her and her eyelids drifted shut.

To her surprise, Ford's lips settled on her forehead. Her lashes popped open only to spasm shut when his lips lifted. Again, she felt the whisper-light touch of his warm breath the instant before his lips pressed gently on her cheek.

His fingers tightened on her waist as his lips pulled away, then moved down to the line of her jaw. Another handful of seconds there and his lips eased down to the side of her neck.

The bolt of hot sensation sent a cascade of paralyzing weakness through her and she felt her knees give out. Ford easily held her up as his lips wandered gently over the tender skin of her neck.

She was clinging to his shoulders now, but her grip was alarmingly ineffective. The only tension her body seemed capable of was the rippling tension of high suspense. He'd not kissed her on the lips, and that worried her. She'd expected that, but not this. Not this warm, almost nibbling exploration. As if he were sampling her skin and tasting her. What did this mean?

Don't you want to know before Friday? A question for them both. A question that implied a test and, even though his small kisses made her shake with pleasure and robbed her of strength, they seemed to be an obvious delay.

Perhaps he'd already determined what he'd wanted to know, perhaps he'd already decided she wasn't suited. And might never be. Maybe he could tell that actually kissing her would be disappointing for him, so he delayed because the idea of kissing her on the mouth was now repellent, or at least undesirable.

Horror sent a dark charge through her that made her legs less shaky. She managed to let go of his shoulders and brace her hands between them to lever herself away, but his steely grip on her waist kept her from creating any better escape for herself than getting him to lift his head.

His dark eyes were heavy-lidded and the harsh look on his face was intense and terrifying. His low voice carried a ragged edge. ''Time's up.''

And then he leaned close and his lips were suddenly on hers, stifling the shocked breath her body drew in. There was no hint of play or hesitance in the heavy mastery of his lips. Rena squirmed a fleeting moment, then was swamped by a wave of heat and sensation so overwhelming that her head spun and her body went slack.

Nothing in her rigid, dim life had prepared her for the shock of his mouth mating so aggressively with hers, probing, invading, then demanding more. His kiss was wildly consuming, firing something so deeply feminine and instinctual in her that she was helpless to control it.

When at last he drew away, she was shaking and in shock, lost in a drowsy daze of pleasure so intense that she could barely focus her eyes. She was clinging to him and her body was so hot and stirred up that she'd all but melted against him.

It was some consolation that his embrace was almost fierce and that he seemed at least as stirred up as she. But his low voice was steady and carried an element of worldly knowledge that let her know he'd not for a moment lost control of himself as she had.

"That answer it for you, Rena?"

Her brain couldn't form a reply. Though she craved some sign from him that he'd got his answer and was satisfied with it, she wasn't brave enough to lift her gaze from his shirtfront to see if she could read it on his face.

Ford had somehow made her kiss him with wild

fervor, virtually turning her into someone she didn't recognize. Suddenly she remembered the small helpless sounds of pleasure and hunger she'd made, and shame struck viciously. She wouldn't be able to bear it if Ford showed any hint of disapproval for those little sounds. It was horrible enough that he must surely think it.

Ford lifted a hand to her face. His hard, callused fingers gently gripped her chin to prompt her to look up at him. She complied, but her gaze shied from meeting his. Suddenly his lips were on hers again, only this time they were gentle and soothing.

The stark craving for more than a gentle, soothing kiss sent another maelstrom of desire and confusion through her. Somehow she managed to allow him to temper the kiss and keep it soft, praying he wouldn't know how much she suddenly wanted more, as if the shame of losing control of herself had not been quite punishing enough for her to want to keep it from happening again.

He'd done something to her, uncovered something she'd never suspected of herself and still couldn't believe. When the kiss ended this time, Ford relaxed his arms and she took a step away, privately appalled as her fingers trailed down his arm then caught his fingers and lingered tellingly before she could make herself stop touching him and let go.

She had to force herself to look at him because

she understood how odd it would be to continue to avoid it.

"Thank you for taking me dancing tonight," she said, comforted when she heard her quiet voice stay steady. "I had a nice time."

Ford's eyes seemed to miss nothing, but there was something fiery and intense in their depths that she might have interpreted as anger until just a few minutes ago. Her fledgling sexual instincts told her that the fiery intensity was desire, but uncertainty about her femininity made her doubt that.

Ford's gruff, "Good night," settled nothing for her, but the moment he stepped into his room and closed the connecting door, she almost fainted with relief. She lay in her bed a long time before her restless thoughts settled enough for her to fall asleep.

CHAPTER FIVE

IT WAS difficult to face Ford at breakfast that next morning. Last night had complicated things between them, and she had no clue to how he'd expect her to behave now.

Common sense told her that last night should have made things feel more comfortable, but life experience had taught her to remain guarded, so she was nervous. And now that he'd opened the door to touching and kissing, how freely did he mean those to happen?

Still disrupted by her hungry response to him, it seemed prudent to try to conceal that from now on. Perhaps the next time he kissed her, she'd have more control over herself. The lingering worry that she might have seemed "too easy" to him was the result of talk she'd overheard from some of the ranch hands. She didn't want to be the kind of female they sometimes talked about, the eager, "easy" kind they liked to sleep with but didn't respect.

And because she didn't truly think she was female enough or refined enough for a man like Ford, she was even more wary of responding to him again as she had last night. Seeming too eager and "too easy" when she was no prize would make her seem needy and desperate to him.

When she walked out onto the back veranda to the table Zelly had set for breakfast, Ford got to his feet and, as he had the morning before, pulled out her chair and gallantly waited to seat her.

At least she'd not awkwardly hesitated to allow it, as she'd done yesterday morning. The polite gesture had startled her then. Ford hadn't seated her at supper the night before because he'd helped Zelly with a tray, so she'd not realized that it was a normal courtesy for him.

The secret pleasure of that and all his other small courtesies—opening doors for her, carrying things for her, serving her first—seemed extravagant to a woman who'd rarely had such things done for her and never realized she should expect them. She considered them small bits of elegance that made her feel feminine and valued, but because Ford was so gentlemanly, she worried that she wasn't lady enough to deserve them.

Rena walked to join him but Ford caught her hand to stop her before she could step between the chair and the table. Her gaze shot up to his in time to see him lean toward her.

"Good morning," he said the moment before his lips settled gently on hers for a slow, lingering kiss. Her free hand came up then fluttered hesitantly without settling. He wasn't touching her at all, except for his lips and his light grip on her hand, so she wasn't certain what to do. The rush of excitement and heat made her crave more, but she managed to keep her response as low-key as his kiss.

When he pulled away, she opened her eyes in time to see the faint crease between his dark brows before she stepped stiffly in front of the chair and he seated her.

When he went around to his side of the table and sat down, she glanced his way, uneasy to see that his dark gaze was searching her face.

"Are you just shy after last night, or are you cranky in the morning?"

The blunt question sent the inevitable burst of heat to her face. She fumbled with the edge of the table-cloth that hung into her lap. "I...feel shy," she said quietly.

Ford smiled then and she was relieved. "Then what do you suppose I can do to help you get over feeling shy with me?"

She stared at him a moment, helpless. "I'm not sure. Maybe in time..." Frustrated with herself, she glanced down and reached for the napkin beneath her silverware to pinch a corner of it as she fought an inner battle.

The truth was always better, though the truth was also very dangerous to speak aloud to anyone, particularly to Ford. But the truth was what was needed now, because only the truth would make him realize how futile all this was. Surely he could see by now that he didn't need that land badly enough to shackle himself to someone like her.

And the word "appeal" bothered her more every time she thought about it. It seemed too fragile a notion to start a marriage with, particularly this marriage. She had to force herself to look him in the eye.

"I'm not good at any of this," she said softly. "I know cattle and horses and hard work, but I don't know what to do with most other things you'd expect in a wife. It took me over a half hour to put on this makeup so I'd get on enough but not too much. That's why I was late coming down. I feel like I'm getting everything wrong, that everyone else knows how to act but I don't. Even when I think I did okay, like last night at the dance, maybe everyone else thinks I blundered. I worry about Friday and everything that comes after."

She paused because she was saying more than she'd meant to and she was suddenly choking on emotion. The rest came out in a rush. "I can't believe either of us will be happy with this deal, not with me like this and you needing a wife not so...ignorant and rough."

Ford had been watching her steadily all this time, his gaze so intent on her that she felt as if he had seen every thought and word before she'd spoken it. Her eyes were drawn by the movement as he lifted his hand and she saw the long-stemmed red rose he held across the table to her.

The fierce sting of tears took her as much by surprise as the rose did and she felt herself go rigid as she tried to hold back. The sweetness of this new gesture struck her deeply and she couldn't seem to help that she reached shakily to take the stem. Ford released it and she pulled the rose close, looking down at it to carefully touch the velvety edge of one petal as she struggled to contain her emotions.

Ford's low voice was gentle. "I see a shy woman who would rather disappoint herself than disappoint anyone else. A woman who hasn't begun to realize her power as a female, but when she does, will wrap this old boy around her little finger as quick and easy as a cotton string."

Rena's gaze shot up to meet the somber sincerity in his. The confusing rush of sweetness and fear made it difficult to speak, and even then her voice was barely above a whisper. "Please don't joke with me."

"I'll always tell you the truth, Rena, always."

"You'd tell me if you were having any worry about this, wouldn't you? If anything I did made you want to stop the deal?"

"I'd tell you."

"W-what about after Friday?"

"I'll always tell you the truth, Rena. Especially after Friday because you'll be my wife."

The sting in her eyes spread to her nose and face as she struggled to keep the pressure of hot tears contained. He was saying all the right things, wonderful things, giving her worries relief, but her very deepest fear was suddenly twisting her up, forcing her to go on.

"And after Friday," she started, hating that her voice was hoarse and whispery, "if you start to think you made a mistake—"

It was incredibly hard to get it all out, so risky and so difficult not to sound pitiable, but she'd become too emotional to find better words. And the fear was goading her now, making it impossible not to pursue this.

"You'd tell me, wouldn't you? Before you started to...hate me?"

The surprise on Ford's rugged face made her gaze shy from his and she was profoundly sick. She clung to the idea that it had been better to ask it straight out rather than let the question eat her up.

Of all her worries and fears about marrying Ford, that one was the worst: that he'd come to hate her as her father did. Because she truly didn't understand her father's animosity, whatever he claimed about her birth causing her mother's death, she had no idea how to prevent Ford from developing the same hateful feelings for her. All she was certain of was that if Ford ever did come to hate her, it would destroy her.

"That's not even remotely possible," he said quietly, but she caught the undercurrent of anger in his low voice and flinched inwardly.

"Lots of things seem impossible at first. Unbelievable. But they happen anyway, even when there's no way to account for them." She found the courage to look over at him again. "I'm just asking to be told if it ever starts, since it's not my chief aim in life to be...disliked. I'd rather we'd part on friendly terms, or as friendly as is possible, with no real harm done."

The faint curve of lips she tried for trembled with the effort and she had to pull her gaze away from the genuine shock she read in his dark eyes. She looked down at the rose, struggling to keep the pressure behind her eyes from doing more than blurring the rich red color.

She'd blundered badly just now, blurting out so much, and she suffered the excruciating shame of having done it. In an attempt to somehow apologize for the mistake that was probably destined to be only one in a long line of egregious mistakes, she made an effort to apologize. She made herself look at Ford, stricken to see his dark gaze searching hers as if he'd only just seen her for the first time. Her heart grew heavier.

"I'm sorry I brought up something to spoil the morning, because it's a fine one," she said. Again she tried something approaching a smile and couldn't do it. "My thanks for the rose. It's beautiful."

After a scattering of silent moments, Ford reached across the table and laid his big hand palm up on the tablecloth. The grim intensity in his dark gaze urged her to respond to him. Hesitantly she put out her hand to his, then felt it swallowed up in a warm, hard grip.

Even now, when she was ashamed of what she'd just revealed to him, she felt that pleasure-fear, that incredible thrill and excitement. It was already impossible for her to be immune to it, to him, and this was only the beginning of the third day. Was there any hope for her or was she already irretrievably lost?

"I mean you no harm, Rena. I wouldn't have made this deal if I didn't think the marriage part could be a success."

She searched his dark eyes, looking for any sign that he wasn't utterly sincere. If he was lying, she wasn't smart enough to see even a hint of it.

"But you'll tell me the min—"

"Loud and clear. But I expect the same from you."

The faint trickle of relief that had started when he'd begun shuddered to a halt. She realized then that her fingers were gripping his tightly.

"It's not my chief aim in life to be disliked, either," he said, "but I hope you'll give me an honest chance."

Wearied by these past days of such emotional upheaval and turmoil, she couldn't begin to guess why he made it sound as if being married to her was important to him. Almost as if getting more land was a distant second to the notion of marriage, though that couldn't possibly be true.

Rena's gaze shied from his. She was relieved, confused, but truly afraid of the warm glimmer of happiness his words caused her. If he would always be this gentle with her, she'd give him any number of chances he wanted, though even she knew better than to tell him that precisely.

"I will," she managed to say.

Zelly came out then with a tray, prompting Ford to release her hand. He stood and reached to take the tray while Zelly put the serving platters on the table.

Their talk over breakfast was more relaxed, and concerned mostly the plans he'd made for Friday, which he brought up for her approval. The quick ceremony she'd first thought they'd have before a judge had evolved into something much more formal and fussy than she'd hoped it would be. But because Ford seemed satisfied with his plan, she was careful about her objections, particularly when he gently scoffed at her worries about the money he must be spending.

Had his deal with her father become public knowledge yet, and if so, how would a big wedding look to people? Wasn't it hypocritical to stage some fancy event when the marriage had a bigger chance of ending in divorce than it did happily-ever-after? Because Ford seemed to know what he was doing and wanted it this way, she hesitated to speak up.

Neither of them had heard from her father, but after learning all Ford had planned and realizing he'd virtually moved heaven and earth and spent a fortune, she began to worry as much that the deal would be canceled as about going through with the expensive public ceremony.

The wedding began at seven that Friday night in the community church in town. The last-minute rush of the day had made her head swim. Ford had met with her father and their lawyers that morning, so the details of the will and the land deal had been signed. Rena's contribution was to go through with the wedding, and she was so nervous that her veil trembled like hummingbird wings.

She managed to swallow her horror when she started up the aisle from the back of the church. The pews were filled from front to back and end to end, and she'd never been around so many people at once in her life outside of high school assemblies in the auditorium.

The sanctuary was a lush heaven of flowers in nearly every color and kind, and mirrored the multicolor bride's bouquet with streaming white ribbons that she gripped so tightly.

Ford stood waiting for her with the minister as she walked toward him alone. Her father had called her yesterday and hatefully refused to be present to see her "make a fancy fool of herself," and she was glad. The ceremony would be difficult enough to survive without having to weather his hostile presence or the public risk of his involvement.

Though the sight of Ford through the gauzy veil softened his ruggedness, he stood tall and elegant in his severe black suit. He looked so formidable and stern and somber, but then he smiled and her heart felt the fragile relief and assurance she'd been praying fervently for.

When she reached Ford and he took her hand, she couldn't keep from hanging on tight. And then the minister began and the solemnity of the moment made an even deeper impact.

The minister thought they were marrying for love, for better or worse, in sickness and in health, till death. Rena was stricken with guilt by the love pledge in the vows he had them repeat to each other, because neither of them had so much as hinted that love might ever be possible. She was certain she was the only one close to feeling it. The words cherish and protect seemed especially poignant, and made her so intensely emotional that she could barely keep her eyes dry.

She'd been able to suppress her tears for most of her life, but standing in this church with Ford, speaking words that held no deeper truth than her secret hope, made her eyes blur dangerously. To her dismay, one tear trembled loose and sent a hot streak down her cheek.

Her hand shook when Ford placed the wedding band on her finger. When the minister finished his charge to them both, they continued to stand facing each other, with her hands gripping Ford's.

"You may now kiss your bride, Mr. Harlow."

Ford released her hands to gently lift her veil. The movement sent a gust of air over her cheek and from the small chill she felt, she knew the wayward tear had not dried. He took her hands again to lean toward her for a chaste kiss, though the heat of his lips lingered after he drew away.

Rena's emotions surged again when the minister finished the ceremony with the Apache Blessing Ford had requested.

"Now you will feel no rain, for each of you will be shelter for the other. Now you will feel no cold, for each of you shall be warmth to the other. Now you are two persons, but there is only one life before you. Go now to your dwelling, to enter into the days of your life together. May your days be good and long upon the earth.''

The minister touched them both and they turned together to face the congregation. ''Friends, I now present Mr. and Mrs. Ford Harlow.''

The rest of those moments in the church went quickly as they walked down the aisle together and waited in an alcove for the guests to leave while the photographer set up to take wedding pictures.

Later, Ford escorted her to his car and drove them to the local restaurant he had rented for the reception.

''You're awful quiet, Mrs. Harlow.''

Ford reached over for her hand and glanced her way with a calm smile. ''You still look shook up. You all right?''

''I'm fine. Glad to get though it,'' she confessed softly as Ford glanced forward to keep track of the drive. ''The church was beautiful, so many flowers.''

Ford squeezed her hand and it was all she could do to keep from putting her other hand over his. The emotion she'd felt in the church was still strong.

They arrived at the restaurant that had been decorated by fat, lit candles, white tablecloths and more gorgeous flowers. They stood together inside as the guests filed past and offered their congratulations and best wishes.

Several of the ranch hands from Lambert Ranch had come to the wedding and the reception, along with Frank Casey and his sons. It made her feel good that they'd respected her enough to show up. None of them remarked on her father's absence. Neither did any of the other guests and she was grateful for that.

The cake was huge and Rena nervously endured the ritual of bride and groom feeding each other a bite of cake. The crowd whistled and hooted with approval when Ford took the bite of cake from her fingers, then caught her hand to return it to his mouth to nibble off a small bit of frosting.

There had been no frosting, and the playful glimmer in his dark eyes as he nibbled her finger broke through her nervousness and startled a giggle out of her. His quick kiss was an obvious reward for the small sound and her affection for him soared.

Whatever others knew about the deal Ford had made with her father, she was certain anyone looking on would think that he was pleased with his bride and that he treated her tenderly.

They danced together to the country band Ford had hired, then spent time with their guests before he determined it was time to leave.

After she tossed her bouquet into the crowd, they

walked through a gauntlet of guests showering them
with birdseed all the way to Ford's car. His big
Lincoln had been decorated with signs and streamers,
and a row of old boots and shoes had been tied to a
rope and attached to the back. Inside, the car had
been littered with more flowers and handfuls of birdseed.

They were going to Harlow Ranch because Rena
had resisted the idea of a traditional honeymoon trip.
She'd worried about Ford spending more money.
He'd allowed her to decide but only after getting her
promise that they'd go on a trip someplace in the
next few months.

Once the well-wishers who'd followed them
through town sounding their car horns had turned off,
Ford stopped his car and got out to reel in the rope
of boots and shoes to stow in the trunk for the highway drive.

When at last they reached the ranch and stepped
onto the front veranda, Ford swept her up in his arms
to carry her over the threshold. But instead of setting
her on her feet once they were inside, he started up
the staircase.

The only lights on inside the big house came from
a lamp downstairs and the one in Ford's bedroom.
Their bedroom now. When he carried her into the
room and kicked the door shut behind him, he kissed
her as he gently lowered her to her feet. She'd taken

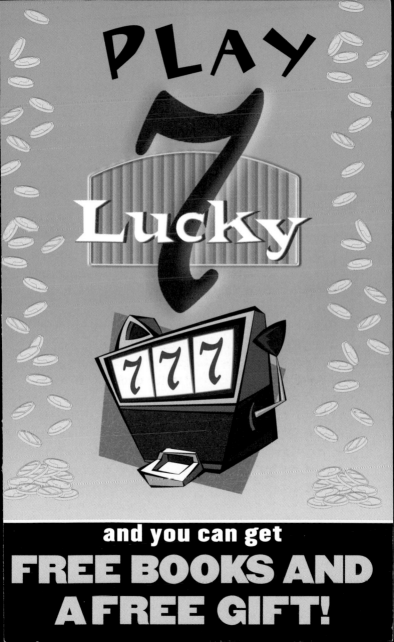

PLAY LUCKY 7 and get FREE Gifts!

HOW TO PLAY:

1. With a coin, carefully scratch off the gold area at the right. Then check the claim chart to see what we have for you — **2 FREE BOOKS** and a **FREE GIFT** — **ALL YOURS FREE!**

2. Send back the card and you'll receive two brand-new Harlequin Romance® novels. These books have a cover price of $3.99 each in the U.S. and $4.50 each in Canada, but they are yours to keep absolutely free.

3. There's no catch. You're under no obligation to buy anything. We charge nothing — **ZERO** — for your first shipment. And you don't have to make any minimum number of purchases — not even one!

4. The fact is, thousands of readers enjoy receiving books by mail from the Harlequin Reader Service®. They enjoy the convenience of home delivery...they like getting the best new novels at discount prices, BEFORE they're available in stores...and they love their *Heart to Heart* subscriber newsletter featuring author news, horoscopes, recipes, book reviews and much more!

5. We hope that after receiving your free books you'll want to remain a subscriber. But the choice is yours — to continue or cancel, any time at all! So why not take us up on our invitation, with no risk of any kind. You'll be glad you did!

We can't tell you what it is...but we're sure you'll like it! A surprise **FREE GIFT** just for playing LUCKY 7!

The Harlequin Reader Service® — Here's how it works:

Accepting your 2 free books and gift places you under no obligation to buy anything. You may keep the books and gift and return the shipping statement marked "cancel." If you do not cancel, about a month later we'll send you 6 additional books and bill you just $3.15 each in the U.S., or $3.59 each in Canada, plus 25¢ shipping & handling per book and applicable taxes if any.* That's the complete price and — compared to cover prices of $3.99 each in the U.S. and $4.50 each in Canada — it's quite a bargain! You may cancel at any time, but if you choose to continue, every month we'll send you 6 more books, which you may either purchase at the discount price or return to us and cancel your subscription.

*Terms and prices subject to change without notice. Sales tax applicable in N.Y. Canadian residents will be charged applicable provincial taxes and GST.

If offer card is missing write to: Harlequin Reader Service, 3010 Walden Ave., P.O. Box 1867, Buffalo NY 14240-1867

BUSINESS REPLY MAIL
FIRST-CLASS MAIL   PERMIT NO. 717-003   BUFFALO, NY

POSTAGE WILL BE PAID BY ADDRESSEE

HARLEQUIN READER SERVICE
3010 WALDEN AVE
PO BOX 1867
BUFFALO NY 14240-9952

NO POSTAGE
NECESSARY
IF MAILED
IN THE
UNITED STATES

off her veil in the car and felt him gently pull it from the crook of her arm as he ended the kiss.

"Do you feel married?" The look he gave her held a glimmer of his earlier playful mood and she liked that.

"It would be hard not to feel married after all that. Everything was so perfect," she said, then suddenly felt worried that both his question and her answer had opened a door for the marital intimacy she wasn't ready for.

Ford carefully searched for the seed pearl comb of her veil and held it up to let the voluminous fabric sort itself out and drape unwrinkled. He seemed to find the veil some small entertainment and it relieved her that his attention had been distracted.

She started to step away to the large closet to change out of the gown, but he caught her hand, letting her know that he'd probably not truly been distracted at all. His voice had gone low, and the playfulness she'd sensed in him was rapidly fading as he gave her a somber look.

"I think I'm going to need help with a few things," he said and she read the message in his dark eyes. "Husbands and wives ought to help each other, even with small things, don't you think?"

She knew instantly that he aimed to start married life with her the way he meant to have it go. Her breath went shallow with dread and excitement. She gave a solemn nod even as her heart prayed, *Please, not this soon.* Surely he didn't expect complete physical intimacy, not yet, but there was no evidence on his rugged face that it wasn't his ultimate goal. *Tonight.*

The knowledge made her heart speed up and she was confused by the contradiction between dread and the obvious excitement she felt. How could she feel both so strongly?

"It's gonna to take a while before we feel completely comfortable with each other," he said then and she felt a tingle of relief. "Four days hasn't been long, has it?"

Rena let out the breath she'd been holding. "No."

"But we're going to share a bed tonight, and I'd rather you weren't terrified."

She glanced away, partly because she wanted him to stop targeting her thoughts, partly because he was so kind that she felt faintly ashamed that she couldn't completely relax with him.

"How 'bout I help you get this veil hung up?"

What sounded like a complete change of subject, wasn't. It was some comfort that she knew it right away, but at least she had a clue to what he'd meant by his talk about husbands and wives doing small things for each other: he meant for them to help each other out of their wedding clothes.

For Rena, it was a huge thing, but in the eyes of

the world and to Ford, it was probably inconsequential. Because she was eager to somehow ease her fears about intimacy, she didn't refuse or try to delay. Perhaps the best thing was to endure it and hope that once she did, she'd feel comfortable with more.

Besides, Ford had been relentlessly kind to her and she felt so obligated to him for her part of the ordinary marriage he wanted, that she didn't believe she should resist him too strongly. His intentions toward her till now had seemed so completely good that she felt compelled to make a good-faith effort to match them. Surely he wouldn't mean to cause her unnecessary hurt or trauma.

And there was also the excitement she felt just being with him. When he kissed her, when he even touched her, she felt a glittering delight that touched her everywhere. She'd be lying to herself if she pretended not to be curious about what sex would be like. Since Ford's touches and kisses were so thrilling, surely complete intimacy would be even more so, wouldn't it?

Rena led the way to the huge walk-in closet. Once inside, she found the hanger for the veil and after it was securely attached, Ford hung it on the rod next to the bag for her gown.

Ford removed his suit jacket and she glanced away to find another hanger. She handed it over and he made quick use of it to hang the garment on the rod next to her veil.

The white silk shirt he wore seemed to emphasize his wide shoulders. Her gaze flashed over the expanse, then slid shyly aside. The sensuality that suddenly flowed heavy and thick between them made her blood begin to pulse.

His voice was husky now, and low. "Could you get these cuff links for me?"

The small request was another gentle descent into sensuality, and when he held out his wrist, she worked the first cuff link out. The second cuff link was removed just as easily. Ford took them and tossed them into the glass tray on top of a row of low shelves. He caught her hand and lifted it to his tie. She froze until her gaze met his and she raised her other hand to begin working the crisp knot loose.

A strange weakness spread through her as the back of her fingers brushed against the white silk, and she became sharply aware of the hard flesh beneath it. The heat Ford radiated in close quarters seemed to both melt her and sensitize her from head to toe. When she'd opened the first two buttons of his shirt and pulled the tie from his collar, she draped the tie across the tray that held his cuff links.

"The back of that gown's got a lot of little buttons," he said quietly, his voice a low rasp. "If you'll turn around, I'll get them for you."

Her knees were already appallingly weak, but she obediently turned, then endured the stark pleasure of his hands as his hard fingers gently worked each button loose. When he reached the end of the row, he stepped close and slid his arms around her waist.

The whisper of silk on smooth satin was a sensual sound that made her blood sweeten and pool. The long moments were heavy with intent as Ford nudged aside the shoulder of her gown and lowered his mouth to the bare skin he'd uncovered. Rena's hands came up to rest on his forearms, and she couldn't seem to help that her fingers smoothed restlessly over the silk fabric, savoring the hard feel of muscle beneath.

She felt dizzy when Ford moved and lifted his hands to her shoulders. The gown began a slow, elegant slide to the floor so she lowered her arms to let it go, her heart suddenly pounding with terror and excitement. She nervously stepped out of the small circle of fabric at her feet.

Ford leaned down to pick up the gown before she could, so she reached awkwardly for a hanger, dismayed by the strange weakness of her body. She hesitated to turn fully toward him. Modesty heated her face, but she forced herself to turn and together they got the gown secured to the hanger before Ford hung it for her.

Without the gown between them, the heat in her

face turned scorching. She made herself look up at him and the dark fire in his eyes sent a flood of shyness through her.

"I don't think I can handle much more of this, Mrs. Harlow, so I'll step out while you dress for bed."

The sternness about him now seemed harsh, but the fire in his dark eyes as they wandered lingeringly over her was somehow a tribute to her feminine desirability and a validation of her as a female. He seemed to be making a strong effort to go about things slowly, but the dark glitter in his eyes gave the impression of barely leashed self-control. The fragile trust she'd come to feel toward him felt even more fragile.

Her soft, "All right," was the best she could do because the rush of fear and excitement she felt was overwhelming.

Ford leaned toward her for a quick kiss before he walked out of the huge closet, closing the door quietly behind him. Rena lifted cool hands to her fiery cheeks, so stirred up that it was all she could do not to give in to hot tears of frustration and agony over her ignorance about what to do now.

CHAPTER SIX

ONCE Rena had gathered her nightclothes and slipped through the side door of the huge closet into their private bath, she quickly showered. When she got out, she used a blow dryer to dry her hair before dressing in the nonrevealing blue satin pajamas and matching satin wrap she'd bought. She cinched the belt snugly around her waist, then hesitated before she stepped out into the bedroom.

Ford not only seemed to have good intentions toward her, but he'd acted on them. But what about her good intentions? If she continued to be so withdrawn and uneasy with him, she risked insulting him.

She was a complete novice at so much, particularly in sexual things, but if she somehow held Ford off until she felt completely at ease, he might never have a true wife.

She could spoil the sweetness between them and virtually guarantee not only the failure of this marriage, but Ford's animosity if she didn't make the same good faith effort for Ford's benefit as he had for hers.

There was nothing abnormal or wrong about a wife having sex with her husband, so if Ford wanted a complete marriage with her to start tonight, she shouldn't resist.

The conclusion brought a knee-weakening surge of dread, but the dread she felt was tempered by a surprising anticipation. Her feminine curiosity was also strong, but a life of reserve and painful shyness made it difficult to think about making herself sexually vulnerable.

By the time she quietly stepped out into the bedroom, Ford was already in bed, sitting with his back against the mahogany headboard, the covers up only as far as his lean waist.

Rena had seen shirtless men before, but they'd been ranch hands working hard on a hot day. To see Ford bare-chested was startling and made her racing heart shift into a faster rhythm. He also must have showered in one of the other bathrooms, because his hair still carried a sheen of faint dampness.

His dark gaze took her in from head to bare toes and a slow smile spread over his stern mouth.

"Very pretty, Mrs. Harlow. Damned pretty."

"Thank you," she said, frustrated by the heavy blush of pleasure his words caused her.

Sexy was the only word for the look he gave her, and her insides were jittery with excitement. Cowardice was tying her in knots, but hadn't she just decided to let him have his way?

His dark gaze followed her every move as she

walked to her side of the bed and took off the satin wrap. Ford flipped the covers down and she shakily climbed into the bed, lying back on the pillow as she reached for the covers.

Ford dragged them over her as he rolled close and braced his fist on the mattress at her waist to hover over her. Just that quickly, he swooped down.

The very carnal kiss he lavished on her left her trembling and clinging to him by the time he ended it. She loved the solid definition of steely muscle beneath his warm skin and she couldn't seem to stop touching him.

He drew back to watch her face closely. "Your hands feel good, Rena. You feel good."

His big palm smoothed up the side of her pajama top, then lifted to the V of the garment. He eased a finger beneath the fabric and gently skimmed the back of his knuckle over her skin. Rena tried not to let her body stiffen at the small intrusion. The fiery intensity in Ford's dark gaze was difficult to withstand, so she closed her eyes.

He leaned down to brush a soft kiss on her lips, then eased back. His voice was low and gravelly.

"You're safe tonight, darlin'."

The gruff affection in his voice made her emotional. Her eyes opened, but she couldn't meet his gaze. Despite his patience with her, she was relieved and that made her feel guilty.

"I'm not very...sophisticated," she said softly and knew right away he would take it as the veiled apology she'd meant it to be.

"I'm satisfied with the choice I made."

Rena looked up at him to see the truth of that as he went on. "There are lots of qualities more important to me than sophistication. Mutual trust is one of the big ones. And I'd rather sex meant something more than it would tonight."

Rena felt a rush of tenderness. She rubbed a hand against his chest, so overcome with affection for him that the gesture had been impossible to prevent.

"Thank you." She couldn't help that the words had sounded as choked coming out as they'd felt.

Ford caught her hand and lifted it to press a kiss against her fingers. "We ought to get some sleep." He leaned down for a long, gentle kiss. Too soon, it was over, and he turned away briefly to switch off the lamp.

Once he had, he turned back to her. "Do you like that side of the bed?"

"It doesn't matter to me." She'd never shared a bed with anyone, so she had no preference.

Ford eased back on the pillow next to hers and drew the covers up. The heat of his big body and the novelty of lying beside him was a surprising comfort. The alienation and loneliness she'd felt for most of her life was suddenly gone, and she lay there in the dark overwhelmed by emotion.

Trust was important to Ford, *mutual* trust. And he wanted sex to mean more than it would have tonight. Her feelings for him began to strengthen and grow. The rest of her tension ebbed away as she thought over the events of these past few days.

The swiftness and intensity of it all still shocked her, but a small part of her began to believe that whatever her father's dark motives had been when he'd offered Ford the bargain, he might have unintentionally set something wonderful in motion.

Quiet and relaxed, she listened to the calm, steady sound of Ford's breathing and basked in the radiant heat of his body until she drifted peacefully to sleep.

Rena awoke slowly that next morning. It surprised her to feel Ford's arm around her. Her head was pillowed on his shoulder and her hand rested on his chest. It felt so natural to wake up with him like this that something wary and mistrustful in her relaxed a little.

Normally she would have gotten out of bed the moment she was awake, but the newness of waking up in Ford's arms and her deep calm about it made her want to savor this a while. She felt closer to Ford than she'd felt toward anyone since her aunt, but it was a precarious closeness that made her want to draw back.

Soon he'd be awake and turn that perceptive gaze on her, and the reserve and control she couldn't help would tie her up while she scrambled to navigate the day with him. Too soon, she'd endure the delicate balance between guarding every word and act, while she tried to decide what the right words and actions were.

She closed her eyes and tried to stay quiet for a few more minutes. As long as they lay like this, she could indulge in the pleasure of feeling close to him and safe. As long as he was still asleep, her insecurities wouldn't be put to the test and the self-consciousness that kept her so on edge would be absent.

The subtle change in his breathing was a clue that he might be waking up, so she carefully eased away from him, slipping from under his arm but taking time to set it gently on top of the covers. She got out of bed and pulled the coverlet back up, then gathered her underwear from a dresser drawer and walked quietly to the big bathroom.

Putting on a bit of light makeup went quickly because of the practice she'd had these past few days. She finished, then stepped into the huge closet to dress.

The bedroom was still silent when she came out,

so she moved quietly across the room to the armchair where she'd left her boots. She'd just sat down and picked up the first boot to put it on, when she noticed Ford rise up on an elbow to watch her.

His voice was rusty and rough. "You remind me of the kid whose friends dare him to walk through a haunted house. The minute he gets outside again and proves he's not chicken, he runs all the way home."

The amusement on his rugged face made her blush a little. He smiled at her and went on before she could think of a reply.

"Zelly'll probably have a tray with coffee and some cups outside the door."

Grateful to have him move quickly past the accurate analogy, Rena set the boot aside and got up to see about the tray. Though Zelly was the soul of thoughtfulness, this was a new little surprise. Her father's housekeepers had never gone out of their way with little courtesies, so it was a novelty Rena appreciated.

When she'd picked up the tray and brought it in, she carried it to the lamp table on Ford's side of the bed. It felt odd to do the wifely chore of pouring his coffee from the server and handing it to him, but she liked it.

Ford moved higher on the bed to lean back against the headboard, so he was ready to take the cup and have a sip. After she'd poured a cup for herself, he gestured for her to sit on the edge of the mattress beside him.

"Is there anything special you'd like to do today?" he asked once he'd tasted his coffee. "We could always run away and have a honeymoon someplace if you've changed your mind."

What she truly wanted to do was to spend the day outside, doing something she knew how to do. She was accustomed to spending the entire day outdoors, often from dawn to dusk, so she'd missed that these past few days. Spending so much time indoors or in malls had made her feel stifled and confined. She was used to hard work, so she'd felt like a malingerer.

"What do you want to do?" she asked, a little uneasy that he'd again brought up the subject of a trip that might cost more money.

"I asked first. What's the one thing you crave to do today?"

Rena searched his expression and reached the conclusion that Ford might have already guessed the answer. Nevertheless, she hesitated to just blurt it out, so she gave a quiet, "I think you know," then took a sip of coffee.

Whether he'd truly guessed what she'd like to do or not, getting him to tell her what it was spared her the awkwardness of a wrong answer if he turned out to not be as perceptive as she'd come to expect.

Ford set his half-empty coffee cup on the edge of

the tray and leaned back to study her face. "I believe that was a small flirtation, Mrs. Harlow. 'I think you know.' Mysterious, a little playful maybe, but guaranteed to put me on the spot."

Rena couldn't quite keep her mouth a straight line. The sparkle of good humor in his eyes was highly appealing to a woman who'd rarely been exposed to playfulness, even as a child.

Ford narrowed his eyes on that faint curve of lips. "Maybe I'll have to use something special to figure it out this time. Maybe use a crystal ball. Have you seen one lying around this morning?"

It was a silly question that made her smile and give her head a shake. Ford picked up her left hand from her lap.

"Ah, here it is," he said, pushing up her ring finger with his thumb in a way that made the diamond on her engagement ring stick up. He pretended to seriously peer into the gem.

Rena was absurdly delighted by that, and didn't try to hold back a giggle. Ford's own smile widened, but his gaze was intent on the ring.

"Hmm. I think I'm beginning to see what you want to do today," Ford went on. "I see a hungry woman and her husband sitting down to a big, hot breakfast. I also see horses, a man and his wife riding someplace, maybe burning off a little energy."

He paused and Rena watched him, very nearly

mesmerized by the sight of rugged, macho Ford
Harlow doing something as frivolous as pretending
to consult her diamond ring like a crystal ball. When
he went on, she hung on every word.

"But mostly, they're just riding around, completely useless because neither of them look like
they're gonna do a lick of work."

Rena couldn't hold back another soft giggle as he
looked at her and lifted his dark brows, prompting
her to confirm his "reading." She set her cup on the
tray, unable to get an inkling of whether Ford was
satisfied with that or not.

"You're very good at...guesses. Is that what
you'd like to do?"

Mischief made his dark gaze sparkle. "Nope.
What I'd like to do is spend the whole day in this
bedroom with my wife. My second choice is to go
outside and get on a horse. It's my guess you're as
tired of the inside of this house as I am."

"You're sure?"

"I'm sure. Did I guess right?"

"You guessed absolutely right," she told him, and
gave him a soft smile. His gaze sharpened on that
soft smile.

"Now it's your turn, Mrs. Harlow. What do you
think I'd like to do right now?"

She felt a strong pulse of sensuality and her smile
faltered a bit. The glitter of mischief was still there

in Ford's eyes, but also something deeper now, and intense.

"Come on, Mrs. Harlow," he growled. "No guts, no glory."

Rena felt a tide of shyness roll through her. He wanted a kiss, and he was virtually daring her to say that out loud.

Suddenly she was impatient with herself. How much courage should it take to let him coax a guess out of her? She liked his playfulness, loved to see his formidable personality soften. If she didn't play along, she could spoil this.

"I think," she began quietly, "that you want a…a kiss." The word was barely above a whisper.

Ford's dark brows went up. "You're sure?"

"Yes." She felt herself relax. It was only a tiny victory over her reserve, but she'd done it.

Ford's smile eased and she caught a hint of his sudden seriousness. "Then give me one, Rena. Kiss me."

Rena stared at him, helpless. Ford had initiated every kiss and almost every touch. Though she was experienced now at kisses, her experience was minor compared to his. When she continued to hesitate, he spoke, his voice going low.

"I know what you're thinking, because it's the same for me. Will she pull back, will she not like it? Can I kiss her in a way that'll make her want more?

Should it be quick, or slow. Light, or deep? Will Rena kiss me back?''

Ford's words were a shock, and his rugged face was now almost grim. She'd never once got the impression that Ford worried about any of that, but he was so solemn that she knew he was telling the truth. The glimpse of vulnerability in him was another mesmerizing surprise. Because he was so strong and confident, it had never occurred to her that she could ever hurt him. Make him angry or insult him, but never hurt his feelings.

His next words were quiet and made her feel a pang of regret for hesitating.

''Do you not want to kiss me?''

''I...want to,'' she whispered, suddenly emotional. Slowly she leaned toward him.

Ford didn't move to meet her halfway. In fact, he didn't move at all. His stillness made her waver a scant inch from his lips. What he'd said about his own uncertainties made another impact on her feelings for him, so she closed that last small space to brush her lips against his.

What began as a small kiss became a series of small kisses. The delectable sensation of kissing him made her lift her palm to his lean cheek as she eased nearer to close the space between her body and his.

The need to give him more, to somehow cause him the same pleasure his kisses always lavished on her—to somehow demonstrate her delight and gratitude for his uncommon tenderness—made her overcome the last of her shyness. She kissed him boldly then, reveling in both his fiery response and the sudden joy she felt.

Ford took over and rolled away to easily drag her across his legs to the center of the mattress. She was suddenly beneath him, but the fiery kiss didn't end until they were both breathless. His voice was a gruff whisper.

"That was some kiss, Mrs. Harlow." He lifted his head to smile down at her. "I'm beginning to think you like me a little."

It was hard to tell if he'd truly believed she might not like him because he seemed to be teasing. But there was something in his dark gaze that gave the clear impression that he was serious.

Her soft, "Of course I like you," was immediate.

"And I like you," he said as his smile eased to a serious line, "very, very much. *So* much," he emphasized softly, "that if we don't get out of this bed right now, one of us is going to lose her clothes."

The remark startled another giggle out of her.

Ford's smile came back. "I like girlish giggles and ladies' laughter, Mrs. Harlow, especially yours."

All at once, he levered himself away, catching her hands to pull her with him as he backed off the bed. The abrupt move had startled her as much as this new demonstration of easy male strength. Surely that was the reason she felt a little dizzy.

"If you'd like to go down and let Zelly know we're ready for breakfast—" he paused to give her a quick kiss "—I'll bring the tray after I get dressed."

Rena left the room after that, pleased with the new sense of closeness between them, amazed at a feeling of joy so deep that she couldn't stop smiling.

They spent the day together. It was good to be out in the sun and the wind, good to be on a horse again. But Ford rigidly steered them away from anything resembling work. Mostly they rode across the land. Ford pointed out landmarks and informed her of the common names he and the men used for different locations, taking time to orient her to the part of Harlow rangeland that was nearest the headquarters. Harlow Ranch was vast enough that further exploration would take days.

Later, after they rode back to the house and had lunch, they went into the den for an afternoon of paperwork. Soon enough, it became clear that Ford meant to familiarize her with everything concerning Harlow ranch business, and the afternoon flew past.

That night, he took her to San Antonio for supper, then a movie. By the time they made the long trip back to the ranch, it was late. The movie, a romantic adventure, had been spectacular.

Rena had never been to a movie at a theater before, but was too ashamed of that to confess it to Ford. She'd had enough to deal with wearing a dress all evening and trying to cope with panty hose. Though they made her feel feminine, they were remarkably fragile, and she wasn't used to having her legs exposed, even with the conservative hemline of her dress.

But Ford's reaction to both the yellow dress and her legs had made it worth the trouble of dressing up and paying much closer attention to her clothing.

Getting ready for bed was another emotional roller coaster of dread and excitement, but tonight her excitement was sharper. In the end, the ease she'd felt with him all day was not strong enough at first to weather the suspense of another opportunity for full intimacy.

Ford made her forget her worries with his first kiss, and this time, when the kisses stopped and he lay back with her in his arms, Rena was so stirred up that she tingled everywhere.

They'd come closer to intimacy tonight. Ford's hands had slid under her pajama top, and he'd gently teased and explored until she'd all but cried out from the pleasure of it. But then he'd stopped and gathered her in his arms to tell her good-night.

She lay awake a long time, frustrated and torn between the need to let him know she might be ready for more, and her ongoing uncertainty about it. She finally fell asleep, but not before vowing to somehow overcome the last of her apprehension so things would end differently next time.

CHAPTER SEVEN

THE next time came unexpectedly at midmorning the following day, and the circumstances were the last ones she would have imagined would lead to intimacy. They'd been out at one of the corrals nearest the stud barn because the new stallion needed exercise and Rena had wanted to watch one of the men put him on a longe line.

But the stallion was particularly uncooperative all the way from the stud barn to the corral, fighting his lead and trying to bully the ranch hand. She'd asked Ford for an opportunity to work the horse herself, but he'd sternly turned her down.

She'd been stunned by his quick refusal. Never in her life had anyone, not even her father, refused to let her work a difficult horse, particularly since the chore routinely fell to her.

Ford's automatic refusal nicked her pride, and the resentment she felt surprised her. She tried not to take it as a slight because Ford had made it clear before that he thought she was good with horses. But in view of her long experience, it was hard not take offense. On the other hand, he knew the stallion better than she did, so perhaps the animal was truly more dangerous than he appeared, however routine his bad manners and lack of cooperation seemed to her.

A second ranch hand came over to help. After a few more frustrating moments of observing the stallion and watching both men's efforts to simply get the animal into the corral, Rena asked a second time.

"He's too dangerous for you."

The words were another little nick to her pride. Ford had seen her catch and calm the stallion just the other day. Granted, the animal had just about worked off his little rebellion by the time she showed up, but she'd done it.

She'd worked with a truly evil horse or two in her life, and the stallion didn't appear to be like either of those. He was surly and poorly trained and had clearly been allowed to get by with bad behavior, but if he'd wanted to do someone serious harm, he was certainly capable of much more aggression than he was showing now.

One of the advantages of being female was that horses who acted up regularly for men regarded her as a different proposition. Curiosity was often enough to get their attention until they realized that smaller size and less strength didn't mean she was a pushover.

The savvy and humane Monte Roberts' method she'd adopted was infallible with all but the most damaged horses, and she believed in the method fervently. Too fervently not to be eager to see how the difficult stallion would react to it.

At last the stallion was in the corral. More frustrating moments passed as the ranch hand clipped the longe line to the horse's halter. Or tried to. The stallion again jerked his head at the last second, then rocketed across the corral.

The red horse circled the enclosure arrogantly, slyly avoiding the ranch hand. The second man ran for a lasso, but the moment he did, Rena turned urgently to Ford.

"Let me have a try with him."

Ford's rugged features were rocky now. "You have a problem with the word no?"

He was suddenly implacable, and it made her realize how little she'd seen of that side of his nature these past days. She'd come to think she'd never again see that implacability directed toward her, so to see it now was truly mystifying.

"I know what I'm doing."

"That's not the issue." His dark gaze cut away from her as if the subject was finished.

Nettled by an anger that surprised her almost as much as Ford's intractable attitude, she pursued the argument.

"Unless it would insult your man, I want a try with the stallion."

Ford's dark gaze swung back to her. Anger and surprise flickered in his eyes. "I don't want you anywhere near that horse. He's too damned dangerous for you."

Her lips parted. "I've worked with da—"

"I said no."

The grim verdict was final. Ford emphasized it by stepping forward and resting his arms on the top rail of the corral to underscore his silent declaration.

His refusal was stunning. Rena stared at his back and the formidable set of his wide shoulders. He was as intractable as the stallion, and the stubbornness about him now was a rude shock.

Ford's refusal to change his mind—to even hear her out—sent her temper soaring. Rarely angry, she was suddenly incensed over this. For days she'd felt ignorant and backward, scrambling to adjust to a new way of life, coping with makeup, dresses, panty hose and social outings, and worrying herself into a state over her inexperience with any kind of intimacy. One of the few things she considered herself competent with was horses, but Ford had diminished the value of her competence by his absolute refusal to consider letting her work with the stallion. He was treating her like a child.

Fury was the only description for what she felt now. The stallion continued to circle the corral, trumpeting a challenge as the other ranch hand arrived with a rope and passed it through the fence to the first one.

The lasso flew toward the stallion's head and dropped neatly around the animal's neck. The rope galvanized the horse, who began to fight it in earnest. The waste of the ranch hand's good effort that, in her opinion, would have a less satisfactory outcome than anyone wanted, made her turn away in frustration and start for the house.

She was too angry with Ford to stay and watch. He'd as much as declared that she would be prohibited from anything he considered dangerous, which would in essence bar her from a hefty share of the ranch work she loved.

But maybe that was what he wanted. Maybe what he truly wanted was a wife who sat around the house and waited for her macho husband to come in from a day of man's work. Whatever he'd said about wanting a wife who loved ranch life, perhaps his true preference was for a more feminine kind of wife. A wife he could take to restaurants and movies and dancing at nightclubs, one who could ride over the land with him when he took the notion or help with his paperwork, but not one who did a man's work with him.

As she stalked toward the house, she knew that probably wasn't true, that she might be overreacting, but the insult she felt over the stallion was sharp. By the time she let herself in the back door and walked through the silent kitchen to go upstairs, she realized that what she was really responding to so violently to was Ford's stubbornness and his refusal to change his mind.

Her father's animosity had scarred her, as had his utter refusal to show her even the smallest kindness. His intractability had so wounded her that any glimpse of it in another man—even Ford—stirred up the pain and frustration and fury of it all.

By the time she walked into the large bath in the master bedroom, she felt teary and hurt. She turned on the faucet and stood bent over the sink for some time, splashing her face with cold water, not caring that the light makeup she'd put on earlier had washed down the drain.

And she was crying now, sobbing like a baby over everything else that had been stirred up. The picture she now carried in her mind of Ford declaring, ''I said no,'' then stepping away to the fence to virtually ignore her, was haunting.

The terror of marrying Ford Harlow was not truly a terror of marrying a stranger or of sexual intimacy, but a terror of suffering another rejection as mysterious and profound as her father's.

And now she'd glimpsed the true potential for rejection in Ford. She'd merely feared it before, but what had happened at the corral seemed eerily prophetic. For him to speak to her like that, to not even let her make her case, then to simply turn his back to close her out, gave substance to her fear.

Weakened by tears, she stopped splashing her face and rested her elbows on the sink counter as her tears and the water ran down the drain. After several moments, she impatiently splashed her face again then reached blindly for the towel.

The fluffy wad of terry cloth her fingers encountered was much closer than where it normally hung. Startled, she glanced toward it and blearily saw Ford holding it out to her. Mortified to be caught crying her eyes out over the sink, she snatched the towel and turned away to press it against her wet face.

"I thought I was alone." She couldn't seem to help that her voice was a bit hoarse. "I closed the door."

"And I opened it."

Ford was remorseless over the small invasion, but it was the steely undertone in his low voice that reminded her of his refusal about the stallion. And stirred her up again.

"Maybe it's good that you're here. We need to talk about how things are going to be." Though she'd made the brisk declaration calmly, she was satisfied by the hint of steel in her own soft voice.

"Maybe we do." His voice was just as calm, but he was terse now, as if she'd just thrown down a gauntlet he aimed to pick up. "And maybe we need to have our talk someplace besides the bathroom."

Rena rubbed the towel over her face, then tossed it to the counter and turned. "The bathroom's fine, because it's a short talk. I've worked with large animals all my life, and I think I'm good at it. I won't have anyone tell me I have to stand by like a fragile flower while men do the work—" she paused "—not even you."

The nervous breath that had created the pause had been impossible to prevent. After a lifetime of silence in the face of conflict, standing up to Ford was difficult to do, even in anger.

And she was terrified of that picture in her brain, terrified she'd fall even more deeply in love with him and suffer the agony of seeing him reject that love and turn his back on her. It was better to prod him into doing it now before she could love him any more than she already did.

Love. The realization hit her like a bolt of lightning. For days she'd struggled not to think in terms as precise as love when she acknowledged to herself that she had feelings for Ford. To have the word manifest itself in her thoughts now was alarming.

And it spurred her on, nettling her to push him, to get him to turn his back on her before she invested any more of her heart.

His dark eyes gleamed with anger and faint shock.

"You'll do what I think's prudent or you'll do nothing."

Rena shook her head to that. "I'm not a child you can order around. I lived with a tyrant all my life, and I won't live with one now."

"Too bad."

The curt words cranked her temper higher. "I decide what's safe for me and what isn't. That stallion is only dangerous until someone teaches him better manners."

"A stallion is always dangerous."

"All horses have the potential to be dangerous. Are you going to keep me away from all horses? What about cattle? They can be dangerous on a good day. I've done ranch work all my life and managed to survive so far."

Ford's gaze was sharp on her. There was real anger simmering in his dark eyes, but the anger churning in her made her unafraid and she went on.

"I won't be the kind of wife who sits around the house rearranging furniture or shopping until you're ready to go out to supper or go dancing. If you wanted some pampered, hothouse flower, you picked wrong."

His handsome mouth was a harsh line. "Are you finished?"

"Did you listen?" she fired back, still angry over

his complete refusal to hear her out at the corral and the wild need to push at him.

A humorless smile quirked one corner of his stern mouth. "Oh, yes, Mrs. Harlow. I heard every word." The humorless smile faded to a somber line. "And I apologize. I didn't mean to hurt your feelings."

It was an amazing thing to say to her and she stared at him. An apology was more than she'd expected. She'd wanted some sort of admission from him that he'd been too restrictive or she'd wanted him to blow up and reject her, but she didn't know what to do about a sudden apology.

And the lingering anger in his eyes was confusing. "You're still angry."

His voice was a near growl. "Hell yes, I'm still angry. I've got a wife I care about who wants to work a dangerous horse."

"I've worked dangerous horses before."

"I know you have. But I haven't had to stand by and watch."

"You watched the other day."

His dark brows went up. "Yes, I did, but what I saw was a lady who's a lot more fearless than my nerves might be able to take."

She gave her head a firm shake. "I know what I'm doing, Ford, I'm not a fool."

"I know you're experienced and I know you're not a fool."

She lifted her chin. "But the answer's still no."

"Today it is. I'm not saying it's a permanent no, but don't expect me to change my mind overnight."

"You're treating me like a child. We live on a ranch. What will you do when you have children?"

"Let's have a couple and see."

The stark statement was another little shock. The fire in his eyes was still there, but it was different now.

Ford pulled off his Stetson and calmly tossed it to the counter next to the towel. After such anger, it was odd to see the measured slowness of the movement. She watched him warily, waiting for him to look at her again. Her gaze swept over him, and for some reason, he seemed like a giant.

And she felt small somehow and overpowered. The anger that snapped in the air carried an undercurrent that sent a whisper of sensual peril over her that she didn't understand at all. The surprise of it made her feel a little breathless.

When Ford looked at her again, his dark gaze was fiery and the heavy sensuality between them suddenly made the air seem thick and heavy. The argument had shifted to something much more volatile and she didn't understand why.

His eyes still carried traces of anger, but the harsh fire there now was desire. She felt her body go a little weak and continued to search his stern expression for a clue to what would happen next.

"We'll take up the subject of the stallion another time."

Rena, still watching him warily, still feeling the peculiar weakness, gave a small nod. "Fine." She started around him but he caught her arm and kept her close. The heat he radiated was partly lingering sunshine, but mostly his alone.

"I want you, Rena. In the daylight."

Her knees went dangerously weak. "W-we're arguing."

"We aren't arguing now. And I meant that apology. The last thing in the world I want to do is hurt you or see you hurt."

I've got a wife I care about. Simple words, magic words. Neither of them had said the word love, but she suddenly felt it too strongly to seriously consider a refusal.

Ford watched her soft profile, saw the faint color flash over her pretty skin. He couldn't explain to her in words why he'd prohibited her from working the stallion, because words didn't seem enough. He was truly sorry he'd offended her and caused her hurt.

But the sudden need to make love to her was harsh and insistent. Dimly he realized that the instinct to make her his, to defeat her frustrating reserve, was some caveman impulse to stake his claim and own her. Ownership was an archaic notion, but the deep male need to establish it now and establish it completely, was goading him, making it impossible to think about letting her walk away to keep herself emotionally aloof another second.

Last night had tested his self-control and he'd known then that he wouldn't make it through another night. Even so, Rena's stunning defiance had blindsided him. He was secretly delighted that she'd stood up for herself, but she'd also stirred him up and managed to demonstrate how weak the bond between them still was. The only thing that could stop him now was the word no.

"I want you," he said again, suddenly unable to find more elegant words.

Because of Rena's virginal sensibilities, he'd expected their first time to happen at night. She'd be wearing that satiny blue and he'd slowly remove it. He'd not expected it to happen in the morning with the sun so bright and them in their work clothes.

But his hold on Rena felt tenuous and insubstantial, and the urgency he felt about it scattered his notions of how the first time should have been. It didn't matter that she'd married him, he knew he hadn't won her. And the feeling he had—that she could easily slip away—made him eager to push this.

Common sense told him that once they made love, her allegiance to him would be permanent and unshakable. The words they'd spoken to each other in the church would be sealed, and their ordinary marriage would truly begin.

Now she looked up at him and he could see her wariness. He could feel her tremble. He took a chance and leaned toward her. The soft kiss he gave her was lingering and he felt the subtle ebb of her tension.

Rena tried to resist the sweetness of the kiss, but Ford turned completely toward her and she couldn't seem to keep from putting her arms around him. But then he suddenly swept her up and carried her into the bedroom. He didn't break the kiss until he'd laid her across the center of the bed and drew away.

She stirred then, lifting her head to see him reach for her boot. Their gazes meant. Ford's rugged face was stony and formidable, but the heat in his dark eyes was anything but anger. Those few seconds moved slowly past and she eased her head back, still staring into his fiery gaze. Her wordless submission made him pull off first one boot and then the other. She closed her eyes and listened as his boots hit the floor.

Self-consciousness and excitement fought their inevitable battle, and though she tried to make her brain function on a rational level, she couldn't. She'd hated what had happened between them that morning.

The craving to somehow breach the emotional chasm between them and the overwhelming need for some sense of security, made her defy her fear of being sexually vulnerable to him.

And it was already too late. She loved Ford and she'd married him. For one of the rare times in her life she didn't want to think past that, didn't want to consider the consequences if he never felt more than lust for her or eventually turned away.

He wasn't an ungenerous man or a selfish or cruel one. In the end, it made little difference. Whether he ever loved her or not, she wasn't strong enough to refuse him.

Ford settled beside her on the bed, hovering over her to brush the back of his finger against her flushed cheek. And then he was leaning down, and she was lost the instant his lips moved masterfully over hers.

She felt the top button of her blouse give as he pushed it out of the buttonhole. His lips moved off hers to her neck and her breath went ragged as he kissed his way down to the opening of her blouse. She felt the next few buttons release one by one.

Slowly, with exquisite care, Ford kissed his way lower. His hand became bolder, hesitating in one place, giving her time to grow accustomed to it, then moving again, ever lower. His remarkable ability to gently explore and yet set each place he touched on fire, short-circuited her fears until she was completely under his power.

She was shaking beneath him and so totally lost in a sweet, heavy ocean of sensuality that there was no going back, no thought of anything but finding relief from the mad escalation of sensation that rapidly became more wonderful and sharp than she thought she could bear.

She didn't care when, one by one, she felt every article of her work clothes slip gently away. Her senses were flooded by the thrill of Ford's hard, hot skin against hers. The small pain that intruded was brief and forgotten in the wild torrent of feeling that, in the end, left her weeping helplessly beneath him, overwhelmed by the most incredible sensations she'd ever felt in her life.

Afterward, her body felt so heavy with drowsy pleasure that she fell asleep in Ford's arms. He dozed, too, until she revived and realized it was almost lunchtime. But her start of surprise and her automatic move to get out of bed was a reminder that she was naked and that her robe was hanging in the closet.

Ford chuckled at her dilemma and gave her a long, sweet kiss. But the kiss had been a distraction for what he'd really planned.

It was one thing to be unclothed in the heat of passion, but quite another to have Ford pluck her from beneath the covers and carry her into the bathroom to set her on her feet next to him in the shower.

His dark eyes missed nothing and she felt her skin go a fiery red as he turned on the water and grinned at her initial attempt to somehow shield herself from his gaze.

In the end, her modesty didn't survive the shower. Which was just as well because when they stepped out at last, Ford grabbed one of the huge bath towels and briskly dried her off. When he handed her a second towel and waited for her to return the favor, she realized the magnitude of the comfort and ease she felt with him now.

She smiled up at him and gamely wielded the towel, giggling when she discovered he had ticklish spots, then laughing when he retaliated. Never in her life had she felt such a sense of companionship and human closeness. The loneliness and alienation she'd felt for most of her life was suddenly gone, and the dark cloud that had shadowed every event of her life was blessedly absent.

CHAPTER EIGHT

THOSE next days were the best of Rena's life. The feeling of friendship between them was both a joy and a challenge. Ford's healthy point of view and common sense sanity made her new life with him as starkly different from her old one as living was from dying. How had she survived so long with her father? How had she endured such enmity and ill will?

And Ford had changed his mind about the stallion. As she'd expected, the animal responded well to her. Ford had watched her every second in the corral, and by the time she put a saddle on the horse and rode him peacefully she'd proved the animal was no more dangerous than any other stallion. She and Ford agreed that the horse needed to have vigorous daily work so he'd focus his energy on something besides mischief when he wasn't standing stud. Ford offered to share the task with her, and it became another joint work project between them.

The social life she'd never had began the night they attended the barbecue at Jenny Sharpe's. The evening went so well that when other invitations began to come, Rena looked forward to them. Jenny invited her into her circle of friends, and Rena actually enjoyed the daylong shopping excursion they'd all taken to San Antonio.

Privately her relationship with Ford deepened, but the troubling truth—that he never actually spoke the word love—haunted her and kept her from completely letting down her guard.

Still flushed with the newness and excitement of everything else, she managed to conceal her lingering fear of disaster. Because she'd focused so much on hiding it, it took a while for her to sense Ford's dissatisfaction. Once she did, some of the newness and excitement dimmed, and she couldn't seem to help that she subtly began to draw away.

It was shortly after that when they were about to leave the house after lunch that she got a call from Frank Casey at Lambert Ranch. She took the call in the kitchen with Zelly nearby clearing away meal preparations and loading the dishwasher.

"Miz Rena, we've got some trouble over here. It's your daddy." The ranch foreman sounded genuinely worried.

"What's wrong?" She'd only talked to her father twice in the weeks since the wedding, and because he'd made it clear he had little to say to her, she'd left him alone.

"He's been holed up in the house the last two days. Won't let anyone in, but you know how he gets. Thought it was because he was in a fury about the housekeeper quittin', but he's up there today making a racket, and it don't sound good. Thought you ought to know.''

"Myra quit?"

"Yes, ma'am. Said he was going through the house takin' everything out of closets and drawers, even down in her room. Said she reckoned it was time to work for someone else.''

Myra was a mostly silent woman who ignored nearly everything but her work. She and Abner had gotten along for years because they rarely acknowledged each other. To learn that she'd quit was almost as surprising as her reason for doing so.

Rena glanced at Ford, who'd just come into the kitchen, then turned away to say quietly. "I'll be over to check on him.''

She'd been about to hang up when Frank spoke. "Before you come over, Miz Rena, you ought to know there's a For Sale sign at the front gate. Musta gone up since yesterday morning, because I didn't see it until just a while ago.''

The surprise of that made her heart fall. Her father had signed a will that guaranteed she'd inherit Lambert Ranch. He'd drawn up a list of bequests to disburse his liquid assets, and her name wasn't listed there. Selling the ranch before it could pass to her would just as effectively disinherit her as he'd originally intended. It was a novel way to both violate his agreement with Ford and yet keep it to the letter.

The hurt that stirred up was still bitter and deep. Old anger came roaring up next and her heart was suddenly churning with the frustration of this new demonstration of her father's animosity.

Why should she care if he'd fired his housekeeper and his behavior had taken another peculiar twist? She fought a silent battle between bitterness and duty, then felt duty slowly win out. However he'd treated her, he was her father. Whatever he was up to now, perhaps it was time to face him a last time. Make certain he was all right, perhaps let him know she was finished with him, then never see him again.

It amazed her to realize that the hope she'd carried futilely since childhood—that her father would one day relent—was still there. It was past time to put a stop to that, to face him one last time and finally let it go.

"I'll be right over," she said softly into the phone. "Meet me out front." When she hung up and turned, Ford was standing a few feet away. She could feel his curiosity and smiled to deflect it.

"I need to go see my father. It shouldn't take long." The words had come out too rushed. "Where will you be?"

"Want me to go along?" The question was mild, but there was an alertness about him that let her know he'd detected her upset. She smiled gently, hoping to counter his perception.

"I'd rather go alone," she said, then added, "if you don't mind." She'd meant to soften her refusal, but realized her tone had been too brisk. She saw the flicker in Ford's eyes and felt a pinprick of pain. The sense she'd had for days, that he was disappointed with her, was suddenly sharp.

And there was nothing more she could do about it. She'd done her best, but perhaps her best would never be enough. Perhaps the dissatisfaction she'd sensed in him was destined to grow, and the disappointment she saw in him now would become too much.

The hurt and frustration of not knowing precisely what it was that was displeasing him or how to do any better made her feel hopeless.

Her father hadn't been able to love her and now perhaps Ford was realizing he couldn't love her either. For all the tenderness and physical intimacy between them, she was starkly aware he'd never once used the word love and neither had she. She knew why she couldn't say it aloud, but she could think of only one reason for Ford's silence.

Suddenly so emotional she had to escape, she said hoarsely, "I need to get over there," then walked back through the house to grab her handbag. Once she glanced through it for her driver's license and checked the charge on her cell phone, she returned to the kitchen and hurried past Ford to go out the back door and rush to the garage for her pickup. She didn't realize until she was on the highway that she'd been too preoccupied to kiss Ford goodbye.

Though she'd known about the For Sale sign, it was still distressing to see it. Rena pulled past the front gate and started up the long driveway. When she was in sight of the house, she saw Frank Casey walking up from one of the barns. Because he was still nearer the back door than he was the front, she stopped her truck near the back of the house and got out to meet him.

"I'm sure sorry, Miz Rena. You want me to go in with you?"

Rena glanced toward the house. "It might be good to have you come in until I see how things are."

What she didn't say in so many words was that she should have a witness. Her father got bizarre ideas, but if he'd suddenly worsened, there was no way to predict what he might later claim about her visit. She was leery of putting Frank in an uncomfortable situation, but there was no help for it.

Together, they started toward the back porch, then opened the door and walked in. Frank pulled off his Stetson and they both looked around. The kitchen was a mess. Dirty dishes, many of them broken, and at least one whiskey bottle had been thrown into the sink. Nearly every drawer hung at least partially open. Cabinet doors stood ajar, and dishes and pans had been pulled out and either sat on the floor or on counters. Broken glass littered the linoleum.

She glanced uneasily at Frank, who looked worried. He went with her as she walked across the kitchen and stepped into the hall. The state of the house was another shock. A lamp that must have been thrown at a wall lay smashed on the floor, and various drawers had been dumped. A heavy recliner in the living room had been turned onto its side, and the coffee table kicked over next to another smashed lamp. Closet doors on the main floor stood open, their contents resting in haphazard piles nearby.

They found her father in the den that served as his office. Stock magazines and books had been pulled from the shelves and left in heaps on the floor. Boxes from the attic were stacked here and there, and the one on his desk sat on its side, empty. Photographs from a shoebox were strewn over packets of papers that must have come from the box on the desk. An almost empty whiskey bottle sat sticking up from the open top drawer of the desk and the smell of whiskey and sour breath hung in the air.

Her father sat bent forward in his chair, his arms crossed on top of the paper mess to pillow his head. His heavy snore was the only sound in the room.

Rena glanced briefly at Frank, who looked shocked. Neither of them spoke as Rena crossed to the desk. She put out her hand to touch her father's arm to gently wake him, but the photographs on top of the papers caught her eye.

She reached hesitantly for one of the photos. She'd seen pictures of her mother, so she instantly recognized the smiling woman in the photograph, though she couldn't begin to guess the identity of the tiny, pink-clad baby her mother held up proudly for the camera. Rena turned over the photograph to read the back.

An odd sickness rose in her chest as she stared at the careful hand lettering: Cissy and Rena at one month.

Frank's low whisper intruded. "Miz Rena? What do you want me to do? Should I try to wake him?"

Cissy and Rena at one month.

Dizziness swept her and she put out a hand to brace herself against the desk. It took her a moment to follow his question, but by then he'd stepped to her side.

"Miz Rena? Are you all right?"

She was too slow to answer, so Frank took her elbow to both support her and get her attention.

"Should I call Mr. Harlow?" he asked urgently. "Miz Rena?"

She struggled to breathe normally and made the monumental effort to clear her head. "I'm...f-fine."

Cissy and Rena at one month.

Outrage flashed through her and she pulled away from Frank to reach determinedly for a handful of photographs. One by one, she shuffled through them and saw picture after picture of her mother and the baby. All the photos, every one of them, were of her mother with the baby—Rena—at different stages of development.

The picture of the grinning baby seated in a high chair included a small birthday cake on the tray. The candle on the cake was in the shape of the numeral one. In that one, her mother was standing solemnly at one side of the high chair and Aunt Irene was smiling into the camera from the other side.

Aunt Irene, her father's sister. The aunt who'd lived with them until her death when Rena was eight. The aunt who'd taken her part against her father and stood up for her. The aunt who'd known her mother hadn't died in childbirth, but who'd kept silent and let her believe her father's lie: that her birth had caused her mother's death.

Anger spiked sharply as she realized what that meant. The aunt she'd loved, the mother figure she'd trusted, had kept silent and allowed her to believe the destructive lie that had tortured her with guilt her whole life. The betrayal she felt was acute.

Abner stirred then, and she looked across the desk as he groggily lifted his head and tried to sit up. As he straightened and thumped back in the chair, his left arm dragged off the desk, pulling a mound of papers to the floor.

He fixed his bloodshot gaze on her. His words were so slurred she could barely make them out.

"What're you doin' here?"

Rena had to fight to keep her temper. She knew at a glance that Abner was still drunk, so there was no point in confronting him until he was sober. She set the snapshots on the desk.

"I came to see what—"

"You wanna see 'er, you'll come home," he declared, his words still so slurred they were difficult to follow. "Tol' you thata million times."

The meaning impacted her and she felt sick. "Who?"

"Who?" he barked, then tried to get up from the chair.

Unable to coordinate the simple movement, he subsided, but his face was purple with sudden fury.

"Who? That damned baby you tried to hide from me, that's who," he railed, "that damned baby you're whinin' after now. You took 'er, and by God I hunted till I found 'er. You want her now, you'll come home!"

Abner swung his right arm, sweeping papers and

photos off the big desk. As he did, the swivel chair moved and he grabbed awkwardly for the chair arm to keep from being pitched to the floor.

Frank rounded the desk to prevent disaster, and once Abner was securely settled in the chair, the old man glanced around as if confused and unable to focus.

Rena came out of her shock enough to note that the left side of her father's face had drooped. His left arm hung heavily from his shoulder and his hand lay limp in his lap. He tried to talk, but his words were now unintelligible.

Frank flashed her a look of distress as he kept a hand on Abner's shoulder to keep him upright in the chair. "We need to get an ambulance."

Rena went numb with it all then. Her fingers felt stiff as she started to reach for the phone and remembered it was lying on the floor. She took the cell phone from her handbag and quickly pressed the buttons for the call.

Her father slumped, so while Frank held him steady in the chair, she cleared a path through the den for the paramedics. She removed the broken lamp and clutter spilled in front of the ransacked chest in the entry hall. On the way back to the den, she grabbed a throw cover from the sofa in the living room to tuck around her father.

The ambulance from town arrived in good time,

and once the paramedics got the old man settled on
a gurney and checked his vital signs, they wheeled
him out. Rena followed the speeding ambulance in
her pickup. Still stunned by the photographs and
what they meant, she didn't recall the swift drive to
the small local hospital once she pulled her truck into
a space in the parking lot.

She caught up with the paramedics in the emergency room and no one stopped her from stepping
inside the cubicle. Rena looked on, her shock deep-
ening as the doctor made official what the paramedics already knew: Abner Lambert had died in the
ambulance.

When Ford caught up with her, Rena was just walking out of the hospital. She didn't see his car until
she paused on the edge of the curb to glance his way.
He pulled up in front of her then leaned over and
opened the door.

She seemed to hesitate as if reluctant to get in,
then leaned down to look in at him. Her blue gaze
met his across the seat and he saw the hollow look
in her eyes. She glanced away and got in, putting on
her seat belt. As almost an afterthought, she closed
the door and Ford was struck by the mental distraction that signaled.

He leaned her way and slid his arm across her

shoulders. That got her attention and she looked at him.

"I'm sorry, baby."

Her gaze dropped from his, suddenly troubled. "I'm not sure I'm sorry. I feel...numb."

He sensed her guilt about that and lifted her hand off her lap to give it a gentle squeeze. "He was a difficult man. It might be easier to sort out how you feel about it once the shock wears off."

"I'd like to go back to Lambert."

The subject switch was evidence of the restlessness he sensed in her. He leaned over and kissed her cool cheek, then drew back and put the car into gear.

Rena hated that Ford would see the shambles her father had made of the ranch house, but her obsession with the photographs and the papers on the desk made it impossible to delay looking through them.

She'd gently suggested that he didn't have to stay with her, but he'd soundly contradicted that. Though his concern for her made her love him more, she was deeply ashamed to have him see the extent of the mess her father had made.

Rena was only a little relieved when he walked in with her, glanced around, but didn't comment. He was at her side for a full tour of the house as she checked for things her father might have damaged or left running that might cause a fire.

The upstairs was also a shambles as was the attic. It was evident her father had not only been in a rage, but he'd been searching for something. When they walked back downstairs, she went directly to the den. Ford came in and joined her.

"I'd like to go through some of these things," she told him, hoping she might yet persuade him to go back to Harlow without her for a few hours.

"Go ahead. While you do that, I'll find a broom and get that broken glass in the kitchen."

"Please don't. I'll clean it up later."

Ford sent her a faint smile. "You can give me a hand later if you're up to it. We've got a couple of hours until we have to get home for supper. Think you can be done by then?"

She glanced briefly toward the desk. "I'll try." She looked over at him to gauge his patience with that idea.

"We can always come back, Rena."

She gave a stiff nod. "There's a broom in the pantry. Unless he put it someplace else."

"I'll find it." Their gazes held another few seconds before Ford went out and she began to organize photographs and papers on the desk into neater piles. She gathered up the snapshots and papers her father had knocked off the desk, then sat down to page through everything.

At first, she heard Ford in the kitchen sweeping

glass, but then her attention was riveted by the papers, some legal, along with a sheaf of papers from a private investigator. She forgot Ford was in the house and was oblivious to the sounds as he moved through the kitchen and started the dishwasher.

Abner Lambert had married late in life to a very young Cissy Cates. They'd been married little more than a year when Rena was born. But the marriage must have already been difficult, because about the time Rena was six weeks old, Cissy had taken her baby and left Abner.

The private investigator's report documented how driven Abner had been to track down his runaway wife.

You took 'er, and by God I hunted till I found 'er, he'd railed that day. Those might have been the words of a father desperate to have a much loved child back in his home if he'd not added, *That damned baby you tried to hide... You want her now, you'll come home!*

The words of a cruel man who'd used a baby to blackmail his wife. Though Abner had clearly been out of his mind or very drunk earlier, every evil syllable fit her father's hateful personality, and Rena believed he'd been mentally reliving the past when he'd said them. The handwritten letters she found among the other papers were heartbreaking evidence that she was right.

Each one of the dozen letters written by Cissy to Abner were the pained, pleading messages of a distraught young mother who'd been kept from her child. It was clear from the wide-ruled notebook paper that her mother had had little money of her own to seek a divorce and even fewer resources to wage a legal war for custody.

What Rena had found at the bottom of the shoebox was just as upsetting. The yellowed newspaper clippings reported the car crash that had killed her mother, but reading her obituary and seeing the words, "She is survived by her beloved husband and daughter," had been particularly bitter to read.

Since obituaries in their local paper were often worded by surviving family members, it meant that either Abner or her aunt had put in the word "beloved." One of them had had the gall to perpetuate the lie that Abner had been beloved of his dead wife, in spite of the proof Rena had just read that he'd treated his young wife hatefully.

No wonder her father had made it virtually impossible for her to make friends and had berated her in ways that ensured she'd have no social confidence to venture far. A quiet, shy child might never find out that the accusation he'd used to hurt and control her—that her birth had caused her mother's death—was a lie.

It was even possible that in Abner's twisted brain, he'd seen Rena's birth as the cause of her mother's death, since her mother had run away so soon after. From the things her mother had hinted at in her letters, Abner must have been rabidly jealous of his wife's affection for her baby. Once Cissy was killed, Abner had been stuck with a child he resented but could no longer use. As Rena had come to believe, there'd been more to her father's animosity than her birth, and now the mystery was solved.

Heartsick, Rena returned the photographs and clippings to the shoebox. She stacked the papers and letters into the larger box before she put the shoebox in on top and folded the flaps closed. Suddenly exhausted, she'd just eased back in the swivel chair when Ford came in.

"Are you all right?"

Her usual automatic response, "I'm fine," wouldn't come. This time, she gave her head a shake and leaned her head back wearily, staring over into his dark eyes.

She wished she had the words and the courage to tell him about the rawness she felt and why. She wished with all her heart that there hadn't been so much hatefulness and evil in her life. The vandalized room around them, this whole sad, grim house, seemed too dismal for a man like Ford Harlow to even see, much less stand in.

But this house had been her home and now, with her father's death, it was her inheritance. However much she'd wanted it before, however strongly she'd believed it was her right to inherit, after learning the truth about her mother and what she considered the betrayal of her Aunt Irene, she could no longer escape the notion that a Lambert inheritance represented something dark and mean.

The sudden craving to go to Harlow, where there was color and energy and light, made her ache. Harlow Ranch was a benevolent kingdom with a beautiful palace compared to this sad house, a kingdom and palace permeated with beauty and peace and sanity, a kingdom where kindness and common sense were the coin of the realm. Ford's home was as much an extension of his inheritance and who he was as this ranch and this house was of hers.

Her gaze shied from the waiting calm in Ford's dark gaze. The vandalized room emphasized the difference between them and the ugly legacy it represented clung to her like a sickness. She couldn't bear to drag it back with her to Harlow Ranch, but as she got quietly to her feet and picked up the box, she wondered if it would ever be possible not to. Would she carry the effects of this cheerless legacy the rest of her life?

Ford relieved her of the box before she led the way out of the room. It touched her to see that the kitchen had been straightened. Ford had taken everything Abner had pulled out of the cupboards and stacked them near the sink to be run through the dishwasher later. Doors and drawers had been closed and the broken glass swept away, which went a long way toward restoring order.

Once they stepped out the back door, she managed to thank Ford, who slid his free arm around her waist for the walk to his car.

CHAPTER NINE

THAT night, Rena told Ford what she'd learned about her mother and her aunt. Her quiet confession afterward about her reluctance to have a funeral for her father must have shocked him, though she saw no outward evidence of that beyond his calm counsel to sleep on it.

He'd been right to suggest that because after a restless night, Rena changed her mind. A graveside service to briefly acknowledge her father's life and mark his death was more respectful than no service at all, and yet she wouldn't feel as hypocritical about that as she would have a more formal service.

Rena felt ashamed to have let bitterness and anger lead her to initially suggest no funeral at all. She was disheartened to realize that her impulse had been a hateful one that her father might have followed through on if the situation was reversed.

The horror of that made her feel restless and sick. Once they'd made funeral arrangements and gone to speak to the minister, they started for the local law office. Her father's lawyer helped settle things with the will and took care of the necessary paperwork for her to inherit.

After all that, Rena's restlessness became acute. They were on their way back from town, nearing the Lambert Ranch road, when Rena spoke.

"I need to go to Lambert and decide what to do with my father's things." She didn't add that she was impatient to straighten up the mess at the ranch house. Ford had made a fair start with the kitchen, but the bulk of it could take days, and somehow it was vital that she deal with it all now.

Ford glanced her way to study her briefly then nodded and faced forward. He seemed so distant. She'd not wanted to let herself acknowledge it last night, but she couldn't escape it now. Ford was subdued, and his silence gave the impression that he was thinking everything over. Reconsidering.

The pain of that made her glance away from his rugged profile. "I probably won't be done for the day till late. Zelly doesn't have to keep meals for me."

"Are you in a rush?"

"It bothers me to let the house sit like that."

She wasn't comfortable confiding any of the rest of what bothered her, so when she went silent, he stayed silent, too. When they reached the Lambert ranch house, Ford caught her hand before she could get out.

"Want some help?"

Of course he'd offer, and that touched her. But she needed time alone to come to terms with everything. "Maybe later."

Rena could tell nothing from the somber set of his face. The opaque depth of his gaze gave nothing away and she felt a fresh nick of pain. There was a barrier between them now. The dissatisfaction she'd sensed in him had become something else, and her complete inability to somehow fix things between them panicked her. The impression that she'd somehow lost him made her feel desperate.

Perhaps she'd told him too much last night, perhaps it had tainted her in his eyes. And how could she find fault with that when she felt tainted? She wasn't brave enough to ask him outright because she wasn't certain she could bear his answer.

Aware that several moments had passed, she glanced away and quickly got out of the car. She walked to the house and couldn't look back as she heard him turn the car in the driveway and start for the highway.

Rena started in the kitchen, clearing clean dishes from the dishwasher before she loaded it again and started it. She began with the downstairs closets, sorting through everything that had been torn out, tossing things that should have been thrown out years ago into piles. The few things that survived the sorting were put back. Later she would give the downstairs drawers and cabinets the same ruthless sorting, but because the afternoon was already waning, she went up to her father's room.

She stripped the bed and left the bedclothes rolled up to launder, then stacked clothes from the drawers that were still serviceable into piles to donate to charity. Other than his clothing and a handful of mementos that she put in a shoe box and set aside, Abner Lambert had few personal possessions, so the decision of what to do with his things was simple.

Rena felt remarkably remote from the task, as if the chore was little more than regular housekeeping. The guilt she felt about that made her feel ill. When she finished, she carried the stacks of clothes downstairs to pile inside the front door until she could go to town for boxes.

By the time she got to the den, she was unusually tired, but the determination to keep moving, to put everything back in order, made it impossible to stop. Rena didn't notice that the sun had set until she heard Ford call out from the back of the house. She put another stack of magazines on a low bookshelf and turned just as he walked into the room.

"You've made progress."

Her soft, "Yes," carried a weary tone.

"Ready to go home?"

The word home made her heart leap and she gave

another soft "Yes." The sudden craving to leave this dismal place and get back to Harlow was overpowering, but the somber look in Ford's eyes once again struck her as remote.

They drove back to Harlow and Rena took a long, hot shower with plenty of soap. The need to somehow wash away her dark feelings about the old ranch house was evidence of the contamination she felt. She'd got her inheritance, but what it represented to her now made it feel more of a burden than a source of satisfaction.

Rena got out of the shower to wrap herself in a fluffy towel while she dried her hair. By the time she'd dressed in her nightclothes and come out of the bathroom, Ford had brought her a sandwich and a glass of cold milk on a tray.

Ford had showered in one of the other bathrooms and was already sitting in bed, paging through a stock magazine. She sat down on the edge of the mattress to make a try at the sandwich. Ford set aside the magazine and leaned back to study her face.

There was still a remoteness about him that made her ache. Her voice hoarse. "Thank you for the sandwich."

She gamely selected a wedge, though she had no appetite. Ford was watching her so she self-consciously picked up the sandwich plate to hold it toward him. "Would you like half?"

His quiet "no" was almost distracted, so she set the plate back on the tray and made herself take a bite of sandwich. Fortunately she'd taken a small enough bite that she got it down quickly, but she doubted she'd get down another, so she set the sandwich half on the plate.

"No appetite?"

Her, "I'm sorry," was automatic.

"You're still in shock." Ford's quiet pronouncement was a small relief. If he understood that, then perhaps he hadn't found fault with her need to work alone that day. Because they'd been virtually inseparable since the wedding except for the day she'd gone shopping with Jenny, she'd been worried that she'd offended him.

"Still worried about the funeral?" he asked, and it struck her suddenly that the aloofness she'd sensed in him had reduced them to short questions and brief answers. He was right about her worry, but not completely right about the cause. It had been weeks since things had felt this awkward.

"No," she said, then added, "guilty maybe."

"Why?"

She instantly regretted the small confession, but perhaps this was an opportunity to somehow overcome the distance between them. "Because it seems spiteful not to have something more than a graveside service."

Ford gave his head a small shake. "The minister will make sure it's a good service. He does a fine job."

"Then...you approve?"

The question was daring, but she had to know. She saw the flicker of concern in his eyes.

"There's nothing to approve or disapprove, Rena. How else can it be done?" He reached over and took her cold hand. "If he had a regular eulogy, what could be said? An outdoor ceremony fits the work he did. We've got someone to sing a hymn and the minister will do his job."

She searched Ford's dark eyes and realized he meant that. Relief rolled over her. Her soft, "Thank you," made her lips tremble with the effort to speak and not cry.

The pressure behind her eyes was almost too much, so she released his hand and stood to pick up the tray. "I'll take this downstairs."

"I'll get it," he said, then threw back the covers and got up to come around the foot of the bed. "Go ahead and climb in."

Rena watched him go and tried mightily to suppress the sting of tears. What Ford had said about the graveside service lifted an awful weight from her and his description of the service she'd planned made it seem practical and dignified.

She took off her robe and got into bed. Ford was

back soon and when he got beneath the covers, he switched off the light.

As he had last night, Ford turned toward her and pulled her against him. The comfort of his hard body increased the pressure behind her eyes. Ford hadn't made love to her last night and when he didn't to-night, the unease she felt increased.

It dawned on her then that there'd been little more between them than touches since yesterday morning. The last time Ford had kissed her had been when he'd picked her up at the hospital. And then he'd only kissed her cheek. It startled her to realize that she'd been oblivious to the loss until now.

And it emphasized the new distance between them. Was he avoiding even the smallest physical intimacy out of respect for her upset, or was this evidence of the dissatisfaction she'd sensed?

Heartsick, Rena laid in the dark a long time before exhaustion caught up with her and she fell into a restless sleep.

The late-morning graveside service two days later went well. Zelly and the ranch hands from both Lambert and Harlow attended the service in the small rural cemetery. Rena was touched when Jenny Sharpe and her father attended, and Jenny's friends also arrived in a show of support for Rena.

Red roses and carnations decorated the casket and

several sprays of flowers had been sent and sat elegantly around the gravesite. The blue canopy overhead shaded the gravesite while the minister read from his Bible and quoted a poem that paid tribute to the Texas cowboy and celebrated a hard life lived close to the land.

The soloist from the local church choir sang a beautiful hymn and the minister said a final prayer. Afterward, everyone filed past her to express condolences. Rena lingered with Ford at her side until everyone left the cemetery.

Ford had invited them all to Harlow Ranch for lunch, but Zelly had gone ahead to supervise the two cousins who would help her serve, so there was no rush to get back. The peacefulness of the old cemetery was calming.

Rena was satisfied by the graveside service and mightily relieved it was over, but she felt guilty that she'd stood dry-eyed and emotionless. Some of the shock of her father's sudden death had worn off, but she was ashamed to feel so little grief for the man himself.

She hadn't buried her father next to her mother, because it felt wrong to do that. It seemed more appropriate to place him in the newer part of the cemetery and now she was glad of it. She'd never been to this cemetery because her father had forbidden it.

Rena had always thought it was because he couldn't bear to think of her mother lying in her grave.

The truth was that if she'd ever defied him and seen the date of death carved on the headstone, she would have known that her birth hadn't caused her mother's death and one of his most effective means of hurting her would have been lost. Perhaps that helped explain her remarkable lack of grief.

She walked away from Ford to the older part of the cemetery. It took her a few minutes to locate her mother's grave. When she did, she laid the half dozen miniature white roses she'd held through the service at the base of the headstone.

The peacefulness of the place made a deeper impression and Rena stood there a long time, letting the quiet seep into her as the sun blazed down and the light breeze eased the worst of the heat. The cheerful twitter of birds and the droning buzz of a nearby bee were the smaller sounds of the outdoors that were too often drowned out by the sounds of livestock and hard work, so Rena found it surprisingly pleasant to listen to them now.

Finally she turned away from her mother's grave and walked toward Ford, grateful that he'd waited patiently for her. Neither of them spoke as they walked to his car. The ride back to Harlow Ranch was just as silent and subdued, and Rena's worries about the distance between them began to steadily grow.

She was relieved when the last of their guests left. Ford had retreated to his den to take a phone call, so she dashed upstairs to change out of her dress and heels into the jeans and T-shirt she'd wear to Lambert Ranch to get back to putting the house in order.

She'd just come downstairs when Ford walked out of the den. His dark gaze flashed over her and noted her handbag.

"Going out?"

Rena caught the faint hint of disapproval. "Thought I'd go over to the house."

"I'd rather you stayed home."

The suddenness and bluntness of that was a surprise. She gripped the handbag a moment, searching his stern expression, at a loss.

"I'd like to get finished over there."

Some of his sternness softened, but she saw the effort he made to do it. "All right. When do you think that'll be?"

"Soon."

The silence that fell then was heavy and she didn't understand why. The awkwardness of it prompted her to explain.

"I'll feel better when I have everything put back in order over there. And I need to talk to Frank."

"No one expects to hear from you today, Rena. You've been working too hard and too long over there."

"There's a lot to take care of."

"Especially when you're doing it alone."

Again she caught the hint of disapproval, but then he went on and his disapproval was unmistakable.

"Why don't you want me there?"

There was a sharpness in his gaze that cut deep and touched something painful in her. Suddenly emotional, she glanced away. The handful of steps between them suddenly felt like miles. Or maybe she wished they were because she didn't want to answer. Nevertheless, she made a start.

"I need to do this...I need to...think..."

Her voice trailed away impotently. She couldn't put it into words, but the urgent need to somehow make sense of the past and sort out her feelings about it was imperative.

And Ford was a distraction, because part of what she needed to make sense of and sort out was her marriage to him. To tell him that in so many words might hurt him, so it seemed kinder to risk his anger.

"All right, Rena," he said grimly and she looked over at him. "I'll give you today and two more, but then you and I need to talk."

His steely tone sent her heart into a sickening slide. Her soft, "Yes, I agree," was hoarse.

They stood silently a few moments, blue gaze locked with black, until Rena was able to glance away.

Without a word, she hurried past him to go out the back of the house. She felt another slice of pain when Ford didn't stop her for a quick kiss. Now that she'd become aware that even the casual kisses between them had stopped, the fact that neither of them offered one this time seemed dismally significant, despite the tension between them.

Rena worked until late that night. When she came back to the Harlow ranch house and walked into the bedroom, Ford was already in bed, reading. She quickly had a shower and put on her nightclothes, then got right into bed.

Ford set his book on the night table. "How'd it go?"

"Well enough," she said, then added, "it might not take another two days to finish."

"Good."

Rena took comfort in that. Ford switched off the light then turned toward her and slid his arm around her waist. The weight of his arm felt possessive, but she noticed he didn't pull her against him as he had every other night since their first night together.

That, too, seemed significant, particularly since there was no good-night kiss. Again.

Real fear touched her then. She lay in the dark a

long time, trying to pinpoint the exact moment she'd first sensed Ford's dissatisfaction with her. It was far easier to try to pinpoint the first sense of distance.

She'd thought it had started after her father's death when she'd told Ford about what her father and aunt had done, and how angry and bitter she'd felt about it. Now she remembered that the first sure feeling of distance had come earlier that day when Frank had called her to report her father's strange behavior.

Looking back, it stunned her to realize how suddenly she'd shut Ford out, declining his offer to go with her. Her physical withdrawal from him had begun then, too. And she'd not been the one to call him later when her father was taken to the hospital. Frank must have done that.

By the time Ford had picked her up outside the emergency entrance, she'd been in shock and distracted by her preoccupation with the photographs and papers she'd seen on Abner's desk. It surprised her now to realize that she'd been nearly oblivious to Ford's presence.

Later, she'd told him the sick secrets of her family and displayed her anger and stark bitterness over it all by confessing that she'd not wanted to give her father a funeral. Though her suddenly remote behavior that day had no doubt been a surprise for Ford, he'd probably been shocked to discover his shy bride was capable of such a spiteful impulse. No doubt it had lowered his estimation of her character. He might now have serious doubts about the kind of person she might turn out to be and she could hardly blame him because it worried her, too.

The compulsion to somehow put her fears to the test made her turn toward him. Ford had said he'd always tell her the truth but she'd not realized until that moment how much courage it might take to hear him speak it to her.

She lifted her hand to touch his cheek, then felt the sudden tension in his big body. Her courage vanished.

"Good night," she whispered, then slipped her fingers away.

Ford caught her hand then leaned close to give her a light kiss before he pulled her against him. "Good night."

The tension between them had been no more than marginally eased. In spite of the emotional and physical exhaustion of these past few days, it took a while for Rena to calm her worried thoughts and fall asleep. But however long it took for her to drift off, she was aware every moment that Ford was still awake.

The fact that they both lay silent and sleepless only increased the raw sense of distance between them.

And she couldn't escape the thought that if Ford hadn't wanted that parcel of land, they wouldn't be lying there now as husband and wife. If he'd not bargained with her father to get it, if she hadn't taken the chance to get Lambert Ranch, her reclusive life would have gone on. Her father would still have died three days ago, and she might or might not have inherited.

Either way, she couldn't deny that if her father hadn't meddled, Ford would have made his life with some other woman. She would have continued on alone for years, possibly to the end of her life, because Ford Harlow would never have been interested enough in his shy, mannish neighbor to come calling.

The sad truth of that weighted her heart with more misery, and she pressed a little closer to Ford to hoard what might be one of her last opportunities to sleep next to him.

CHAPTER TEN

BECAUSE she hadn't slept well, Rena got out of bed before first light and silently dressed. However quiet she'd tried to be, Ford woke up before she got her boots on and rose up on an elbow to watch her. Neither of them spoke until she murmured a soft, "I'm going on downstairs," and left the room.

Breakfast was just as silent until Rena drank the last of her coffee and stood. When she did, Ford did no more than briefly glance her way and she felt a nettle of anger.

All her life she'd believed she'd caused her mother's death. She'd lived with that guilt and had been tormented by the idea that her life was something she had to apologize for, as if she'd somehow stolen the air she breathed and the small space she took up from someone more deserving of life than she.

This was the man who only a few short weeks ago had handed her a rose and said the most wonderful things before he'd taken her hand and pledged to always tell her the truth. He'd helped her begin to change her feelings about herself, but now he seemed to have given up on her.

"Having second thoughts?"

The question was out of her mouth before she let herself consider the consequences. Her rare temper was suddenly running hot and it was mixed with a feeling of hurt that was surprisingly acute.

Ford looked over at her, his dark gaze as stern as the set of his rugged face. "I'm not happy right now."

"Have you given up on me?"

Ford leaned back to study her. "Running out of patience maybe," he said briskly, then added in a low voice, "but if you expect me to give up on you, be prepared for a long wait."

Those words and the steel beneath them reached out and gripped her insides. The hard glitter in his gaze underscored it all, but the harsh set of his face confused her and made her wary of what he'd meant.

"And I didn't just set an arbitrary time you can extend later, Rena," he went on. "I meant two days. Today's one."

She ignored his dictatorial tone. "Are you... sayin—"

"What I have to say to you will wait until tomorrow night." Ford nodded toward the drive where her truck was parked. "Maybe you need to get going."

She stared at him a moment more, her anger gone, but she didn't understand any of this. He said he hadn't given up on her and that gave her hope. But he wouldn't talk to her until tomorrow night and he seemed impatient for her to leave.

Her confusion must have shown because his voice dropped even lower. "That's right, Mrs. Harlow. You think about this. Settle what you can about your daddy and how you used to live, then think about what you're gonna do now and how I fit into it."

Mystified but encouraged, Rena stepped off the veranda and angled across the patio to walk to her pickup.

Frank Casey and his sons were hardworking and honest, but the thing Rena had admired most about Frank was his affection for his sons. Beau was twenty years old and Bobby was twenty-two. Frank had been widowed when the boys were quite young so he'd had the chore of raising his sons alone. The house and wages he'd got on Lambert Ranch had been enough to make a home for the boys, and Rena knew the three of them had saved money for years in hope of one day buying a small place of their own.

As she pulled up to the back of the Lambert Ranch house, Frank was just walking up the lane from his house. The boys were running to catch up with him and Rena watched as she switched off the engine.

Beau reached his daddy first and snatched off the older man's battered Stetson. Bobby caught up and promptly rescued the hat to cram it down none too gently on his father's head.

Frank chuckled and reached up to straighten the hat and prevent another theft. "Sure glad you boys are feelin' your oats this mornin', because you gotta long, hot job on that south fence line."

The exchange was a frequent one. All three were good-natured and companionable with each other. Frank's sons idolized him and he was proud of them. He took their hijinks with good humor and had never been above a gentle prank of his own now and then.

Rena had envied their closeness and she watched them thoughtfully a few moments more before she reached for her handbag and got out of the truck. Frank came over to outline the day he'd planned and Rena thanked him before she went into the house.

The moment she walked in the door, the dismal feeling of the old house dragged her heart low and she set her handbag on the nearest counter. As usual, the unhappiness of the past seemed to permeate every room. Though she'd boxed up all her father's things and carted them to town to donate to the church, she still felt his surly presence. After witnessing another episode of fun and affection between Frank and his sons, she felt it more sharply than ever now.

Most of the work she'd intended to do here was finished. She'd told Ford it might not take as many as two more days to deal with it all, but as she

walked through the grim house she began to reconsider that.

Rena made a quick tour from the main floor to the
attic, then came back and sat down on the front stairs
for a few minutes. She'd realized yesterday that she
hated this house because she hated what it represented to her. And yet it wasn't fair to blame the
house. It was solid and well constructed, with enough
space to raise lots of children in, though no Lambert
ancestor she knew of had ever had many children.

As she sat there, she tried to imagine it with a
different look, perhaps with softly colored walls in
different rooms instead of yellowed white, and new
carpets. The bathrooms could use the updating the
kitchen had had a few years back, but everything
could initially benefit from fresh paint and perhaps
new drapes. Some of the furniture was so old it could
be replaced.

The decision she'd come to had an element of risk,
but the moment she made it, the oppressive feel of
the old house began to lift. Rena got to her feet and
started back to the attic. She lost track of time then
and the longer she worked, the more certain and
driven she became.

Rena also began to sort out her thinking about her
father and her aunt. It was reasonable to consider that
her father had been mentally ill. And it made sense
to her after some thought that perhaps the reason her

Aunt Irene had kept the secret about her mother might have been because Abner had threatened her.

She remembered Abner frequently shouting at Irene, and he'd always made it clear that Irene only got to live on the ranch because she was blood kin and had nowhere else to go. Other than the fact that Irene cooked and cleaned for him and took care of Rena, Abner had never seemed to care much for his sister.

God only knew what her Lambert grandparents and great-grandparents had been like if their line had come down to a hateful, crazy man like Abner and a sister who'd been dependent on his goodwill. But they were both gone now and Rena was the last Lambert.

The sudden sense she had, that the past was finished and she could make the future go another way lifted her spirits. And that made her think about Ford. What would the future hold with him? Did she truly have a chance for real happiness or was she doomed to eventually make even worse mistakes that would finally spoil it all?

The knowledge that she'd already made mistakes and that she and Ford were at odds, made her impatient to find some way to fix it. Because the situation had gotten away from her before she'd realized what she'd done, she had little confidence about preventing the same thing from happening again.

But at least Ford would give her a chance.

Running out of patience maybe, he'd said, *but if you expect me to give up on you, be prepared for a long wait.*

Her heart lifted higher.

I'll always tell you the truth, Rena, always.

Remembering those things was some comfort, but she was terrified of taking Ford's good intentions for granted. Just because Ford meant well wasn't necessarily a guarantee that he would be able to follow through. He was a man of his word, but how far could she expect his word to go if she continued to disappoint him? Particularly if he discovered he couldn't love her.

Rena tried to set her worries aside for a while, but they hung on. She was grateful when it was time to go down to the cookhouse for lunch. Eating with the men was a welcome distraction as she listened to what they'd accomplished that day.

Afterward, she asked Frank and his sons to come up to the house. She had Bobby and Beau carry the boxes that held her mother's belongings to the cab of her pickup, then had them take out the dozen or more boxes she meant to donate to the church.

While they handled the chore, Rena had a talk with Frank and made her proposal. Frank heard her out and agreed, so when the boys came back inside, Rena repeated her proposal for them.

By the time she left the house to start for town, the boys' enthusiasm had invaded the old house. The love and camaraderie of the Casey's had already lifted the oppression in the dim rooms and Rena knew she'd made the right decision.

She dropped off the boxes at the church, then drove across town to the hardware store. Once she'd loaded the first of the paint and paint supplies she'd bought into the back of the truck, she drove to Lambert Ranch.

Frank and his sons had already started preparations for the massive interior paint job, and once they'd unloaded her pickup Rena started for Harlow Ranch, her heart pounding with fear and excitement.

It was nearly three-thirty by the time Rena arrived at the house. Zelly told her that Ford was in the den doing paperwork, so Rena asked her to keep her arrival secret. Rena pried off her boots then rushed quietly up the back stairs for a shower. Afterward, she put on fresh makeup then went into the huge closet to decide what to wear.

She hadn't worn the pastel pink sundress she'd bought, so she took the hanger off the rod to hold the dress up for inspection. The fitted bodice had a hidden band of wide elastic around the top because the sundress had no straps. She'd bought it on impulse the day she'd gone shopping with Jenny and the others, but she hadn't dared wear it because she felt in constant peril of it somehow sliding down.

The soft pink fabric made the dress look sweet and feminine, but the strapless, fitted bodice made it sexy—or at least as sexy as Rena's reserved nature could dare.

The feminine instincts that Ford had repeatedly validated told her the dress would please him. And if he was pleased with the dress and the effort she'd made to wear it for him, then perhaps it would be easier to breach the distance between them.

Rena was standing in front of the mirror to give the bodice a couple of tugs to test the security of the elastic, when she remembered the time Ford had set. He'd given her two days but she was ready for their talk a day early.

She briefly considered the wisdom of waiting, but it boiled down to this: could she stand the suspense of a longer wait? She'd missed the closeness between them and missed even more the affection they'd shared.

Though there were no guarantees that trying to straighten things out with Ford would restore the closeness and affection between them, she couldn't wait another day for things to be settled.

Resolved, she picked up the white sandals she'd bought to go with the dress, then set them aside. Ford seemed to enjoy seeing her barefoot, and since putting on the dress and making this effort was meant for his enjoyment, she took a nervous breath and started out of the closet to slip downstairs.

When she was outside the open door of the den, she stayed out of sight and waited for Ford to finish his phone call. She gripped her hands together nervously then unclenched them and made an effort to relax. She took a moment to check her reflection in the glass of a picture frame, then heard Ford say goodbye and hang up the phone.

Saying a hasty prayer for success, she tried for a neutral expression then stepped into the open doorway. Ford hadn't noticed her, so she put out a shaky hand and rapped her knuckles softly on the door frame.

Ford glanced up and his distracted gaze sharpened. She walked quietly into the room until she stopped a few feet from the desk. Though Ford's stern expression didn't alter by so much as a flicker, his dark eyes practically devoured her. She felt encouraged and her heart began to slowly lift.

''Nice dress.'' His terse comment was followed by his subtle inspection of the fitted bodice.

Rena felt her face heat because she didn't own a strapless bra. She'd thought the fitted bodice concealed that, but she'd obviously underestimated Ford's male savvy about how the lack of one article of clothing might make a dress look.

"Thought I gave you two days." Though Ford's voice was curt, it had gone a little hoarse.

Rena walked closer to the desk, pleased when he watched her every step of the way. "You did. But I'm done with the house now. Or at least until Frank's ready to start some of the bigger improvements."

"When will that be?"

She got the impression that although Ford had asked a question, the sundress was still his primary focus.

"It'll take them a while to repaint." Rena took a breath once his dark eyes came up to hers. "I told Frank I wanted him and his sons to live in the house. After they move in, Linc Fuller can move onto the ranch with his wife if he wants to, and they can have the house the Caseys use now."

She managed to get it all out, and knew the moment Ford realized the significance of what she'd done because his gaze searched hers. He leaned back in the chair and lifted his dark brows.

"Sounds like you burned some bridges."

Rena could barely breathe. That's exactly what she'd done. If things didn't work out with Ford, she'd have no place to live on her own ranch unless she bought a trailer. She doubted she could bear the cost of building a house for herself this year.

But whether or not things worked out with Ford,

she didn't only mean to change things at Lambert Ranch, but she meant to change herself. She finally found the courage to answer his remark about burning her bridges.

"You might…be stuck with me."

Ford's stern expression didn't change, though she caught the bright spark in his dark eyes and instantly recognized the playful glimmer.

"Stuck with you, huh?"

Rena made an effort to match his playfulness. "I…like it here. I'd like to…stay on."

She wasn't as good at play as Ford, but if she could have another chance with him, she'd learn to be.

"I hear you're a hard worker," Ford said evenly, "but I've got enough people working for me. What other reasons could you give to keep you around?"

His voice had softened and gone low with the question, and her heart quivered with suspense because beneath the illusion of play, she knew he was serious. She tried to find the courage to say the words she'd already committed herself to say. Though her insides were going wild with anxiety, she tried to keep her voice from trembling.

"D-do you have enough people around who… love you?"

Her breath caught as she saw the glimmer in Ford's gaze flare to a hot blaze.

"No," he said thoughtfully, still playing along as if he were mentally reviewing a list of employees, "can't say as I do."

The tension between them was taut, but she was determined to continue as long as she could in a playful vein. There was some protection in that because if she said it playfully and he rejected it, she might not be as devastated as she would be if she'd made her confession seriously and more directly.

"I think if I stayed around," she said, trying to defeat her sudden breathlessness, "I might be able to love you enough that you wouldn't need many other people around to...take care of that...chore."

Ford's stern lips twitched, but he managed to keep them a level line. The fire in his eyes went higher. "When I think about taking someone on for a job, I usually like to see how they do with the work." He paused and his voice dropped to a growl. "Come here."

Rena walked around the desk, her knees shaking so much now that she thought they'd give out. Ford slowly turned the swivel chair so he was facing her by the time she got there. He tilted his head back to look at her and the formidable set of his features gave way to a slow, sexy smile.

"I surely do hope you'll take shameless advantage of me Miz Rena," he drawled, and the emotional distance between them vanished. "Because it's been so long since I've felt loved that I reckon it has to be at least five days since I've had a really fine soul-shakin' kiss.''

Because she still couldn't quite banish that last scrap of shyness, Ford held out his hand. Rena reached for it and he pulled her down to his lap. She slid her arms around his neck and his free hand dropped down to smooth up her bare leg past her hemline to her thigh.

Rena's response to that was automatic and she leaned close to put everything she had into a fiery kiss. Though Ford had welcomed her, she was aware this might be the most important kiss of her life.

Seconds later, Ford took over completely until she was limp in his lap and they both struggled to breathe. Even then, she couldn't seem to stop kissing him and pressed kiss after kiss on his lips as if she'd never get enough.

Ford's hand wandered higher and he was the one who suddenly broke off the series of kisses to speak.

''Well howdy there, Miz Rena,'' he said with a wide grin. ''I think you forgot to put on more than your shoes and a strapless whatchamacallit.'' He grinned at the heat in her face. ''I don't think I can remember a time when a lady showed such an intense level of interest in my affections.''

''I hope not,'' she said, her voice a trembling

whisper. "Because I love you too much to ever think of sharing."

Ford's grin suddenly dropped and after a quick heartbeat, he pulled her close for another fierce kiss. The hunger in it this time was so wild and uncontrollable that she was close to tears. She'd missed this, missed the incredible feelings and sensations, missed the closeness. She'd been so starved...

And she'd managed to confess her love for him. Though he hadn't said the words to her in return, this was so wonderful it could only mean that what he felt for her was at least close.

Ford broke the kiss and caught her chin to hold her steady for a long, penetrating look into her eyes. "I love you, baby, every minute. Maybe from the first day you came here and let me know you didn't want to marry for land."

He paused again and his face went utterly somber. "I should have told you that a long time ago, but didn't think you'd believe it. Or worse. That you didn't trust me enough to love me yet."

He gave her a slow, tender kiss. "I was wrong to wait. I was beginning to think I'd lost you."

I love you. The words she'd ached to hear from him and had worried so deeply about. And he'd loved her from the first. The miracle of that sparkled sweetly through her and for the first time in her life she felt loved and felt it profoundly.

"I love you," she said, helpless to say anything else, so thrilled to say it to him that she couldn't stop smiling.

Ford gathered her in his arms and stood, then hesitated for another kiss. This one he kept moderate and brief before he started around the desk with her and strode out of the room.

They were a half hour late for supper, but Zelly didn't remark. Tonight she'd put the candelabra on the table and flowers in a cut crystal bowl. Ford got out champagne and once they'd settled everything between them and began to make plans, they toasted their future.

It was two years before they welcomed the first of the children they would have, and when they'd finally finished having babies eight years after that, the number had reached four. Neither of their sons and neither daughter were ever aware of anything dark or unhappy in the past, because the life they had with their mother and father was solid and loving. The Harlow legacy was one that welcomed and healed, and one day their children would do their part to continue it.

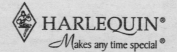

Strong and silent...
Powerful and passionate...
Tough and tender...

Who can resist the rugged loners of the Outback?
As tough and untamed as the land they rule, they
burn as hot as the Australian sun once they meet
the woman they've been waiting for!

Feel the Outback heat throughout 2002 when
these fabulous authors

Margaret Way
Barbara Hannay
Jessica Hart

bring you:

Men who turn your whole world upside down!

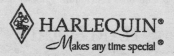

Visit us at www.eHarlequin.com   HRTA

Liz Fielding

Winner of the 2001 RITA Award for
Best Traditional Romance, awarded for

THE BEST MAN
AND THE BRIDESMAID

Coming soon:
an emotionally thrilling new trilogy from this
award-winning Harlequin Romance® author:

It's a marriage takeover!

Claibourne & Farraday is an exclusive London department
store run by the beautiful Claibourne sisters, Romana, Flora
and India. But their positions are in jeopardy—the seriously
attractive Farraday men want the store back!

It's an explosive combination…but with a little bit of
charm, passion and power these gorgeous men become
BOARDROOM BRIDEGROOMS!

Look out in Harlequin Romance® for:

May 2002
THE CORPORATE BRIDEGROOM (#3700)

June 2002
THE MARRIAGE MERGER (#3704)

July 2002
THE TYCOON'S TAKEOVER (#3708)

Available wherever Harlequin® books are sold.